The Courtship

The Courtship

STORIES BY
BUDGE WILSON

Anansi

First published in 1994 by
House of Anansi Press Limited
1800 Steeles Avenue West
Concord, Ontario
L4K 2P3

Canadian Cataloguing in Publication Data

Wilson, Budge
The Courtship

ISBN 0-88784-550-9

I. Title.

PS8595.I5813C68 1994   C813'.54   C94-930054-3
PR9199.3.W55C68 1994

Cover Design: Brant Cowie/Art Plus
Cover Illustration: *Deco Dancers* by Rod McGrattan, Charlottetown, P.E.I.
Typesetting: Tony Gordon Ltd.
Printed and bound in Canada

The following stories have been previously published, in somewhat different form: "The Courtship" in *The Pottersfield Portfolio,* vol. 11; "Elliot's Daughter" in *The Pottersfield Portfolio,* vol. 15, no. 2; "Mrs. MacIntosh" and "The Canoe Trip" in *Islands in the Harbour,* Lockport, N.S.: Roseway Publishing, 1990; and "The Dress" in the University of Windsor Review, vol. 26, no. 1.

The author would like to thank the Canada Council for their generous assistance during the preparation of this book.

House of Anansi Press gratefully acknowledges the support of the Canada Council, Ontario Ministry of Culture, Tourism, and Recreation, Ontario Arts Council, and Ontario Publishing Centre in the development of writing and publishing in Canada.

This book
is for
Sharon McCue

Contents

The House on High Street   *1*

The Courtship   *13*

Elliot's Daughter   *39*

Mrs. Garibaldi and Leonardo   *59*

Mrs. MacIntosh   *87*

The Canoe Trip   *103*

The Losers   *117*

The Dress   *123*

Janetta's Confinement   *141*

THE HOUSE ON HIGH STREET

WHEN VIRGINIA WAS in her mid-forties, she started thinking about the past — her own past. Up until then, she'd just moved from one part of her life to the next, without looking back very much. But then, all of a sudden, without any real warning, she started to care about those things in her life that were finished. She didn't know why this happened. It just did. Maybe there was a part of her that began to suspect that nothing is ever finished. Perhaps she watched her two children and started to wonder about her own childhood. Or possibly she could feel herself sliding downhill in the direction of old age and felt that someday she might need some memories to explain who she was and where she had come from.

One day, she sat down for a second cup of coffee after Jeff and the girls had left for work and school. She loved this part of the day. The early morning confusion was over — the mislaid pencils and notebooks, the lost car keys, the nagging over breakfast choices, the general air of flight — and the rest of her work had not yet begun. She looked out the kitchen

window at the bright May morning, and thought, This is the kind
of weather that Mum always chose for our annual trip to Dartmouth. She always said it was a pity to waste a ferry ride on a rain
storm. And why go in the winter, when it's too cold to enjoy the
outer deck? No. She'd look out the window on a morning such
as this, and announce, "This is the day. It's fine, and it's Saturday,
and it's time we went." Nobody needed to ask her what she
meant. They knew. They were going to Dartmouth to see the
old aunts and uncles. In the house on High Street. Virginia's
father was spared. On the day she was now remembering, he
went off to collect his fishing gear, well satisfied with this turn of
events. But Virginia and her brother always joined their mother
on this particular expedition. "Hurry!" she said. They rushed
upstairs to change into their very best clothes.

Virginia is up in her bedroom looking in her closet, trying to
choose between her two Sunday dresses. "Your blue velvet with
the collar," her mother calls out. "That's the one to wear. They
haven't seen you in it yet." Good. She always loves wearing it.
It is a deep rich blue, and the collar is made of white lace. Her
hair is long and straight and blond, and she knows that she looks
pretty in this dress. She does not put that thought into so many
words, but when she has finished dressing and looks in the
mirror beside her pink bureau, she likes what she sees smiling
back at her from the glass. She wears long beige stockings, held
up by garters from her white cotton vest — called a *waist*. The
stockings itch the back of her knees, but she's allowed to wear
her patent leather shoes with the straps. This makes up for the
itching. It is 1936.

Her brother, Ian, is looking less pleased. He doesn't like dressing up, and he's feeling uncomfortable and silly in his stiff clean
clothes. He has a lot of curly blond hair, and he's thinking that in
the fancy shirt he's wearing, he looks like a girl. He hates that.

Ian is ten years old. Later on, Virginia will remember his age, because this is the month when Freckles O'Brien will die of polio. None of his friends will ever forget that time. They will fix events according to whether they happened before or after Freckles' death. In that year, they are not grieving for Freckles so much as they are agitating over their own mortality. They become hypochondriacs for a while, fearful of germs, aware of what a headache may signify, their minds cluttered by visions of wheelchairs and braces. Infantile paralysis, they call it. Not polio.

If Ian is ten, then Virginia must be eight. She loves going to visit the aunts and uncles. She enjoys their eccentricities and their flaws. And when they return home, she will take pleasure in her mother's spirited account of the day to her father. Virginia's eyes are always wide open, watching, and yes, her ears are flapping.

The ferry ride is, as always, wonderful. They park the car in the vehicle lanes, and then climb the steps to the middle deck, from which they watch their departure. The breeze is cool, and Virginia sits down on one of the benches close to her mother, hugging her coat around her. Ian wanders all over the boat, inspecting things — the life preservers, the wheelhouse, the tangle of mysterious machinery.

Some Dartmouthians ride on the ferry every day, but for most Haligonians, a ferry ride is a major adventure. Huge gulls are riding the wind, far up in the sky, and fat little tug boats are chugging down the Harbour towards George's Island. The water seems to be full of vessels — large and small ones — and Virginia marvels that they do not bump into one another. Then she remembers that once, nineteen years ago, two ships did precisely that. And the collision and resulting explosion wiped out one third of the city of Halifax, as well as inflicting terrible destruction on Dartmouth. What would it have been like to be on the ferry that day? She shivers, and pulls her coat even more tightly around her.

"Cold?" her mother asks.

"No," she says. "Just thinking."

When they drive off the ferry and start their journey to the house on High Street, Virginia starts thinking about what lies ahead. She imagines the aunts and uncles standing at the doorway, ready to greet them — old, deaf, and very interesting. The house will loom up above her like a storybook mansion, its eaves and verandas trimmed with a profusion of Victorian carvings and curlicues, its yellow paint shining in the sun. From the front lawn they will be able to see right out to sea, past the islands and all the way to the horizon.

It is almost exactly as she has imagined it. As the car rolls into the circular driveway, the heavy front door opens, and the four of them are standing there, their hearing aids sprouting wires that connect to the round amplifiers decorating three of their chests. They are shouting at one another and at their visitors; the air is alive with voices, warm with smiles. Virginia is so delighted to watch all this that she forgets to check the horizon for ships.

When she enters the front hall, she is once again dazzled by its size and contents. Each year it is both familiar and surprising to her. The gleaming surface of the mahogany staircase rises in front of them, and a dark red carpet marches up to the second floor, held down by polished brass rods. A lamp on the newel post is lit, although it is ten o'clock on a sunny morning. The rose-coloured glass shade is held up by four scantily clad young maidens, made of some kind of dull metal. The drapery that they are wearing covers most of the embarrassing places, but its arrangement looks loose and precarious. One of the metal maidens has a bare breast. Virginia looks at it very carefully, and thinks that she'd like to touch it. Will it be round like her mother's, or pointy like Aunt Gloria's? It's a bit too high up for her to be sure. Virginia is not an authority on breasts, having seen her mother and Aunt Gloria naked only once — in one of the little unpainted bathing houses on Hubbards Beach.

Aunt Melissa is short and stout, but very erect and puffed up. She has wiry white hair and an unbeautiful face, dominated by an overlarge nose. It is clear that she is in charge, so it would appear that nothing has changed. She is telling everyone where to go — into the parlour — and she is ringing a little silver bell, ringing and ringing, to summon the maid with the tea. Virginia sits down carefully on one of the brocaded chairs, secretly running her fingers over its silken surface. All around her are precious and exotic things — especially the brass clock on the marble mantle, whose pendulum turns and then turns again, with a lazy and mesmerizing movement. She looks at the Dresden figurines, the ornate silver candlesticks, the fringed lamp, the lace curtains, the velvet pincushion, the carved wooden footstool. She loves and she covets almost everything she sees. The room smells of deeply embedded dust and stale face powder. Ian looks uncomfortable and unhappy, but Virginia feels no pity for him.

Aunt Melissa's husband is Uncle Hal, and Virginia likes him the best of all. He is tall and uncoordinated, bumping into things, tripping over the edges of scatter rugs. She remembers this about him, so she watches him carefully, noting that he's still doing it, still bumbling around. However, he is the only one of the four who hears at all well. He seems a gentle and kindly person, and finds a stereoscopic machine for Ian to look through at a set of three-dimensional pictures. Although Virginia does not care whether or not Ian is happy, she admires Uncle Hal's sensitive hospitality. He obeys all of Aunt Melissa's shouted instructions ("Get Ida a more comfortable chair, Hal!"

and "Go tell Minnie to hurry up with the tea!" and "Stop fidgeting, Hal!"). But mostly he just stands in front of the fireplace as though warming the seat of his pants, smiling at the three visitors, shifting his weight from one long leg to the other.

Virginia wonders who owns the house. If it belongs to Aunt Melissa and Uncle Hal, why do Aunt Melissa's sisters and brother live here, too? This seems odd to her, but intriguing. Or maybe it belongs to the family, to the MacIsaacs; if so, it is Uncle Hal who is the hanger-on, the person who doesn't quite fit. Virginia feels a vague pity for him, perhaps because he is the only one who is quiet. The others are all shouting at one another.

The sister and brother here are Auntie Hester and Uncle Sherman. Auntie Hester is small and mousy and solemn, her grey hair drawn back from her face in a scraggly little bun. But her features are regular and firm, and Virginia decides that she may have been very pretty when she was young and didn't have all those lines in her face. She is not married. Once Virginia asked her mother about this, and she said, "She was in love once, long ago, but it didn't work out." Virginia looks upon her as a tragic figure, like a princess in a fairy tale who has been thwarted in love. As Auntie Hester moves about obeying Aunt Melissa's various commands, two tendrils of curly hair come loose from her severe hair arrangement, and lie along each temple. With that sudden softness, her old face reveals what must have been there forty-five years ago. She is slender and graceful in her simple navy-blue dress, and wears a velvet band around her wrinkled neck.

Uncle Sherman is red-faced and blustery, full of loud pronouncements — on the weather ("This will be a long hot summer, mark my words!"), women ("They're far too full of themselves, nowadays!"), politics ("Anyone's crazy who votes for the Liberal party. Damn Grits!"). His wife is in a sanitorium with TB, and has been there for over thirty years.

The tea is wheeled in on a teawagon by Minnie, starched and stiff in a black and white uniform. It is passed around in delicate China cups, one of which has butterfly wings for a handle. Virginia's desire to own this cup is almost physical in its intensity. She and Ian get milk, in small manageable glasses. They're careful to set them down on the coasters provided. There are three plates of assorted small cakes, arranged on a three-tiered silver contraption, and Ian perks up a bit during this part of the visit.

On the whole, much is said, and little is listened to. Maybe, Virginia thinks, this is because no one can hear properly. Or perhaps for other reasons. However, she is an avid listener. She hears everything, and tucks it all away for future consideration. Sitting there on the embroidered chair, she categorizes her aunts and uncles. Aunt Melissa — the bossy one; Uncle Hal — the sweet one; Auntie Hester — the sad one; Uncle Sherman — the angry one.

Once Virginia asked her mother what they all did with their time when the three of them weren't around to be entertained. What did they do with the three hundred and sixty-four other days in the year?

"They play bridge," she said. "And scream at one another."

"Because they can't hear?"

"Well, yes. And also because they all have terrible tempers. All the MacIsaacs, that is. Auntie Hester looks so meek and mild, but when she plays bridge something comes over her. Mostly she just *looks*, but if you got in the way of that look, it could kill you." She laughed. "Heaven help anyone who plays the wrong trick. I'd rather put my head in a noose than play bridge with that bunch."

"If they're so cranky, why do you visit them?"

"They're family."

"How did they get to be family?" Virginia pressed, not understanding her reply.

"They're my father's brother and sisters."

"Did he have temper tantrums, too?"

"Yes."

"Was he deaf, too?'

"Yes."

"Will you get to be deaf sometime, too? And bad-tempered?"

Her mother paused. Finally, she said, "I had a mother as well as a father. I'm not entirely locked in by my genes."

Virginia couldn't tuck that one away in her head. She didn't understand any of it.

✳

When Minnie comes in to clear away the tea things, Virginia knows that the time has come. They will go upstairs now, and visit Aunt Adelaide. They will also go to see Benjamin. Virginia has been looking forward to this ever since she changed into her blue velvet dress. But now that the moment is at hand, she can feel a familiar hollow sensation in her chest, a confusing combination of delight and dread.

They visit Aunt Adelaide first. Her sisters and brother are very hard of hearing, but Aunt Adelaide is stone-deaf. Virginia tries to imagine a life of total silence, but her imagination cannot take her that far. Aunt Adelaide is also arthritic to a degree that Virginia has never witnessed in any other person. Her hands are misshapen and fixed, as solid as a statue's. All of her that is visible — her face, her fingers, the skinny ankle that can be seen below her afghan — looks like a wax doll. She can move almost nothing, but she can manage to flip over a page. She reads and sleeps. That is all. Virginia's mind is agape with fascination and horror. Auntie Hester is the one who looks after Aunt Adelaide, the one who bathes her, brings her books from Miss Bell's lending library in Dartmouth, feeds her, does all the necessary bathroom things. Virginia tries not to think about the details.

Aunt Melissa writes Aunt Adelaide a note. "Here are Ida and Ian and Virginia."

Aunt Adelaide offers a stiff and toothless smile; her eyes are glassy bright.

"Hello," Virginia's mother writes. "How lovely to see you."

More notes pass back and forth, and Aunt Adelaide manages a shallow nod, smiles, and speaks in a high strained voice — barely audible, and to Virginia, unintelligible. She has on a frilly white nightgown, blindingly white, and a mauve shawl protects her narrow shoulders. Auntie Hester must have dressed her like a doll, thinks Virginia, lifting each rigid arm and then setting it down again. An afghan covers all the rest of her — except for that waxy ankle that protrudes indecently above the woolly slipper. Virginia does not take her eyes off her for one instant. She can hear Ian's heavy breathing behind her.

Next they go to see Benjamin. Auntie Hester and Uncle Hal don't stay around for this version of Show and Tell. Benjamin is Aunt Melissa and Uncle Hal's son, their only child. Virginia does not know what is wrong with him. He is a fully grown person, but he is lying curled up on his side, with the sheet pulled up over his shoulder. Virginia can see that his neck is long and thin and very white. If you look carefully, you discover that he is tied to the bed by a very long cloth strap fastened to the bedsprings. He has handsome features, but it is hard to decide how old he is. Maybe thirty-five years old. Perhaps forty-five. But he looks much younger. His eyes are open, but he is focusing on nothing.

Everyone speaks to him, Aunt Melissa and Uncle Sherman shouting, Virginia's mother speaking quietly, but they all know he cannot understand any of it, and that he will not reply.

Benjamin frightens Virginia, but he also interests her enormously. She doesn't know where the fear comes from, but it is real, and she feels it deeply. She believes that if Benjamin suddenly looked up at one of them and said, "Hello," she'd have nightmares about it for the rest of her life.

One day, about a year after this visit, Virginia gathered up the courage to ask her mother why Benjamin was the way he was. Her mother didn't answer right away, but apparently she decided that Virginia was old enough to know, because she told her.

"When he was born he was perfectly normal," she said. "Or so I'm told. I never saw him when he was an infant. Uncle Hal had a position in Bermuda for a while. That's where Benjamin was born. It was in Bermuda that they all started living together. They thought it might cure Uncle Sherman's wife, but it didn't."

"But what about Benjamin?" prompted Virginia.

"Oh yes. Well. They all came back when Benjamin was about ten months old. One day when Aunt Melissa was carrying him into the garden, she dropped him on the flagstone path. She must have tripped or something. He's been like that ever since." She frowned. "What a tragedy for Aunt Melissa and Uncle Hal," she said. "All those years."

But on this day, Virginia doesn't know any of those interesting details. Benjamin is a mystery, and she wants to watch him a little longer. When Aunt Melissa and Uncle Sherman are outside showing them the garden, she slips away and reenters the house by the back door.

Climbing up the mahogany staircase on the silent carpet, she pauses in the little alcove at the top of the landing. She can hear Auntie Hester and Uncle Hal talking, and she doesn't want them to know that she's up here being nosy. She peeks around to see where they are. Their backs are to her, and they are standing in the doorway of Benjamin's room. Uncle Hal's arm is around Auntie Hester's shoulder. She is standing very close to him, touching him with the whole left side of her body. She says, "He was such a beautiful baby."

Uncle Hal looks down at her, and smooths a strand of hair away from her forehead. "And still is," he says. He speaks very quietly, and she cannot hear him. She's as deaf as the rest of them.

"*Ours*," says Auntie Hester. She whispers this, but she spits the word out, and Virginia can hear her very clearly. Auntie Hester leaves Uncle Hal and goes into the room, adjusting the covers, smoothing the sheets over Benjamin's humped-up body, tucking him in. Then she touches him gently on the side of his face.

When she turns to leave the room, her face reveals a mixture of grief and rage, terrible in its intensity. Virginia hears again her mother's words: *If you got in the way of that look, it could kill you.* But Virginia is not in the way, nor is Uncle Hal.

When Auntie Hester reaches him, he looks down at her for a long time. Then, as Virginia looks on in amazement, he kisses Auntie Hester upon the lips.

Virginia once saw the girl next door when she returned home with her boyfriend after a dance. They stood on her veranda in the full glare of the outdoor light, and kissed. The kiss lasted for such a long time, that when they did it again, Virginia counted, "One-and, two-and, three-and . . ." She got to thirty-five before they drew away from one another.

❋

When Auntie Hester and Uncle Hal kiss, it isn't just a friendly peck. No. It's exactly like the kiss of the girl next door and her boyfriend. Virginia finds herself counting. She reaches thirteen, and then they stop.

Virginia's astonishment makes her feel vacant and weak. Her legs are like chunks of putty, but she tiptoes across the landing to the back stairs and goes down quietly. Her head is so full of questions that she needs to find some place where she can be alone, in order to think about the answers. She lets herself out the side door, and goes to sit in a small gazebo at the edge of the garden. Virginia stays there in the little summer house for a long time.

❋

Virginia looked down at the table and saw that her coffee had not been touched. The cup was cold. But outside, the morning was still bright, and the air very clear. Through the trees and beyond the grain elevators, she could glimpse the intense blue of Halifax Harbour.

"Yes," she said, speaking aloud in the empty room. "It was a day exactly like this one."

No wonder Virginia remembered that year so clearly. Freckles and his death. Benjamin and his life.

THE COURTSHIP

MR. VANBUSKIRK SAT on his veranda, rocking. He lifted his eyes — heavy-lidded and remarkably sexy for a man of eighty years — and looked upon the day. "A day like any other day," he mused aloud. But he was wrong. It was not.

Down the street, Mrs. Knickle, who slept better than Mr. VanBuskirk, opened her eyes and observed the bright June morning, watching the mottled light dance upon her ceiling. Reaching out to a glass on her night table, she dipped slender skilful fingers into the water and fished out her teeth. Popping them into her mouth with a delicate expertise, she smiled quietly, her face transformed. Next, she cupped her hands and placed all eight fingers and both thumbs under her hairnet, lifting it carefully from a profuse but untangled mass of chalk-white curls. No blue rinse here, but a very expensive wash-and-wear perm from Les Cheveux, last Thursday. She patted her curls gently and could feel that the spring had survived the night. Putting on a pair of rimless glasses, adjusting the curved metal sides around her ears, she checked her watch. Eight o'clock. She counted on her fingers, moving her lips. Nine hours. Subtract the hour in the middle of the night, which had followed a trip to the bathroom. Eight hours. Very good. She smiled again, somewhat smugly. No one else in her peer group could boast of eight hours' sleep every night. Over coffee, they spoke of insomnia, the late show, night prowling, and discussed "dwindling need." Nonsense, thought Mrs. Knickle. She needed that eight hours. In fact, she felt that very few of her needs had dwindled.

Reaching down under the covers, Mrs. Knickle smoothed her blue nylon nightgown (gift of Mary on Mother's Day of a year ago) over her spare body. As her hands passed over her thighs, she frowned slightly. Lank shanks. Somebody had said that, some writer, a poet maybe; her memory had become so unpredictable of late. The phrase hung in the air. She felt it had something to do with age, and she knew it was not a compliment. Mrs. Knickle was seventy-seven years old.

As was her wont when faced with an unpleasant fact, Mrs. Knickle looked at it as briefly as possible, and then averted her gaze, switching her channel to a better picture. She tested her resting heart rate, pressing the carotid artery in her neck and counting the seconds on her wrist watch. She tipped her head in order to accommodate her bifocals. Sixty-two. Very good indeed. Her brisk, daily two-mile walk was paying off. Mrs. Knickle stretched and flexed the muscles of her thin arms and legs. Almost no arthritis, despite that week-long period of damp Nova Scotia weather. She continued to smile at the shivering dappled ceiling. She was ready. For the day, and for whatever else might present itself.

Slithering out of bed with catlike agility, Mrs. Knickle stood erect, pulling her five-foot-one-inch form up to its full height. She padded quickly out to the kitchen on bare feet, and made herself a cup of tea. Bringing it back to the bedroom, she placed it on the night table and plumped up three fat pillows. Then she climbed back into bed. Looking out the east window at the sparkling new day and drinking her tea, she decided to plan strategy. Mrs. Knickle had not lost the habit of hope. Cheerfully and tenaciously, she clung to the custom of expectation. For example, she *expected* each morning to receive a letter in the mail. She applied this outlook to almost all of her life. She was about to do this now.

One of the pleasures of living alone, she thought, as she took another sip of tea — postponing strategy for a moment — was that you could do, in private, all the things frowned on by society. As, for instance, with the slurping of one's tea. She slurped contentedly. Belching was also permitted in a world that contained no one to hear it. And other censored things. She chuckled into her tea. Basil had been against just about everything. Against noise (gastronomical, musical, social, conversational, and the kinds made by children), Irish Catholics and socialism. Also underdone meat, laziness, and Mrs. Knickle's predilection for the colour purple. She had loved him and mourned him; but she remembered the morning when she first emerged from her loneliness and grief to sniff the heady scent of freedom.

It had been, of all things, a bleak November day, with the rain pouring down in wind-driven sheets from the northeast. She had looked out at it and addressed her canary. "When I was a child, I loved just such a day." Then she had suddenly stood up a little straighter and looked about her with a kind of wonder. A soft, surprised warmth spread through her chest cavity. There was no one there to speak of sloth, no one to make disparaging remarks about her choice of reading materials. She could do it. She could read all day if she wished. Plato's *Republic* or a trashy novel. Take your pick. Quickly she had laid and lit a fire in the living room, brewed enough coffee to last the day, crawled back into her housecoat, and read for six hours. At noon she had taken a small glass of sherry, sipping it slowly. Then she had planned the rest of her life, as she looked out the window at the driving rain. "We could need another Ark before this storm is over," she had said aloud, "and if there is one, I mean to be on it."

That was ten years ago. She had been sixty-seven then, and young. Seventy-seven was not old, she mused, but it was undeniably moving in that direction. Ten years, she felt, is long enough to be free. She had been sensing a niggling urge, of late, for companionship — companionship of the kind that only a husband could give. She wanted someone who was always *there*, not someone you called and arranged to meet for lunch, or a person you dropped in on for coffee. She was starting to crave a live-in presence to whom she would be Number One. Who would listen to her theories about life or to her informative and unmalicious gossip about the citizens of the town. Who would cherish her diffuse general chitter-chatter.

A good cook, she longed for someone with whom she could share her excellent meals. Basil had always relished her cooking, and had told her so. He had been as opposed to ingratitude as he had been to noise and purple and Catholics. He had also been against dishonesty and cruelty and the depredation of the forests. It is true that he had sometimes been dishonest with *himself*, and could be cruel without even knowing he was doing it. And consistency had not been his strong point. It was during his presidency of the local Committee for the Reforestation of Our Country that he had cut down her favourite dogwood tree without even consulting her. He was a horticultural snob and felt that dogwood was a lower-class tree. Furthermore, he had just simply assumed that she would agree with his point of view. Her frequent comments over the years on the dogwood's beauty (blossoms, leaves, berries) had apparently slid past his ears, unperceived.

Basil had been opinionated and domineering, but Mrs. Knickle had to concede that he had grown up in an environment that fostered this kind of nonsense in men. And it was one of the sad facts of present-day feminism, she felt, that it had created, fully-armed, as it were, a host of opinionated and domineering women out of what had been a lot of rather nice people. The old order had been bad, certainly, but what it had yielded to was sometimes not much better. Some women, she had observed, solved their problems by simply placing themselves on the other side of the seesaw. She was ready to move back to an area of middle ground.

She had intended to plan strategy, but she found herself continuing to think about Basil. If one chose, one could shove most of the blame onto Basil's mother for bringing him up to be so pushy. But in the long haul, it had been she, Mrs. Knickle, who had let the results of his mother's training prevail. She could, she knew, have stood up for Catholics, eaten rare beef, and worn purple. But she had simply switched her emotional channel on and off for thirty-five years. She had walked around Basil's offending attitudes when she should have been kicking them into the corner. But the time for fretting about this was long past.

She enjoyed good memories of Basil. He had adored her in his own way, had found her beautiful. Shortsighted in so many other areas, he had also failed to see that she was too short, too thin — indeed virtually without any shape at all — and that her features (described by some as birdlike) were uncompromisingly sharp. He had been good in bed; and at times of extreme pain (when Mary had rheumatic fever, when Chuck had that awful car accident in high school, each time one of her canaries died), his comfort had been sustaining and generous. All things considered, and given the temper of the times, Mrs. Knickle felt that it had been a good marriage.

And now she had had her fill of independence, of widowhood. It was 1984. Time was passing. She wanted someone else in that house with her. She wanted a person to snuggle up to in bed, to enjoy her *coq au vin*, to ask about her day. She also suspected that she was at least slightly in love.

Four houses away, Mr. VanBuskirk rocked back and forth on his veranda. Between his own spruce tree and the house across the street, he could see the harbour glistening in the early morning sun. A good town to live in, he reflected. Never more than a quarter-mile from the sea. Or a lake, or some kind of water. "I could not survive without water," he said aloud.

"No one can," said a cheeky voice from the sidewalk. Ogden Johnston faced him from the bottom of the veranda's wooden steps. "The teacher says no one can. Not even people who are *young*. So it must be extra important for *you*." Ogden was eight years old.

Mr. VanBuskirk looked at Ogden's bland face. "I wasn't

talking about that kind of water," he said coldly. "I was referring to something more spiritual. Something more aesthetic."

"My brother has asthma, too," Ogden said. "But he doesn't talk to himself. You do."

Mr. VanBuskirk chose not to reply.

"My mother says it's a real bad sign to talk to yourself," Ogden continued.

"I almost never talk to myself."

Ogden had been raised to believe that it was a virtue to express himself. His mother was a painter, and his father wrote bad poetry. "You do so. I hear you. Often. Behind the screen door. Talking and talking."

"Probably on the telephone, or calling the cat. And why?"

"Why what?"

"Why is it a bad sign?"

"I don't know. I'll ask my mom. Then I'll let you know." Swinging his antique Yo-Yo, taking care not to step on any sidewalk cracks, Ogden walked crookedly down the block to his house. He lived next door to Mrs. Knickle.

✳

Mrs. Knickle saw Ogden enter his house, banging the screen door behind him. She wondered, as she had done for over fifty years, why children found it necessary to slam doors, while most adults simply shut them. It was one of the few things in life that irritated her. She frowned, and made a mental list: slamming doors; chewing food with one's mouth open; drying dishes too slowly; removing nail polish with one's teeth, with accompanying scraping noises; all forms of nose picking. And dogs that yap.

Clucking at her current canary on her way to the kitchen,

Mrs. Knickle made her breakfast and readied herself for the day. For one whole hour she had let her mind wander from the matter at hand. Strategy.

She was too old for the hard-to-get approach. That procedure called for youth, when you had all the time in the world in which to lay the groundwork. Of course, subtlety would be required, just as it was in all exchanges between people. The direct slam-bang system almost never worked, and she had always been far too pragmatic to use methods that were not practical. No. She would assess Mr. VanBuskirk as best she could, and then work out a way — slithering sideways — to walk straight into his heart.

Mrs. Knickle's knowledge of Mr. VanBuskirk was sparse. He had moved into his house on Spruce Street five years after Basil died. He was a retired university professor — of what, she did not know — and she assumed that his mind must therefore be full of profundities and intricate sensitivities. This appealed to her. Basil had been a dedicated laboratory technician whose conversation had not been stimulating. Her family had felt that she had married below her intellectual level; but he had had marvellous cheekbones and massive shoulders, and she had not listened to their counsel.

Mrs. Knickle's contacts with Mr. VanBuskirk had consisted of "hellos" and "good mornings" as one or the other of them had passed by. Or when they met on the bus. She had always enjoyed observing his long lank frame (in a different category entirely from lank shanks) as well as his bedroom eyes — enormous, brown, with what she felt was a lingering regard. Shaded lids. Hiding complicated thoughts; telling nothing. Eyes to be reckoned with.

Then Mrs. Knickle had attended a community meeting to protest the building of a high-rise factory structure directly beside the town's public park. Mr. VanBuskirk had arrived, clothed in a highly becoming MacGregor plaid shirt; he also had worn a pair of jeans that had shown off his flat stomach. She had looked around at the paunches with which she was surrounded. Ogden's father, only thirty-five years old, had a stomach that lopped over his belt, almost obscuring it. Their town councillor, Mr. Wesley Rankin, sported chins as well as stomachs. The men must have outweighed the women, four to one.

At the meeting, Mr. VanBuskirk had sat down, hands placed on his knees, perfectly still, speaking to no one. Mysterious, thought Mrs. Knickle. Enigmatic. He doesn't look unfriendly. He just looks . . . contained. Then, when Mr. Gilbert Hogan rose to discuss progress and business acumen in connection with the new factory, Mr. VanBuskirk got up slowly from his chair; he stood tall, still, dignified — no fidgeting, no tics — and addressed the gathering. Mrs. Knickle envisioned him in a toga. She fitted him with a laurel wreath and then discarded it. The plaid shirt kept intruding, and his hair was wrong.

But his speech. Oh, how she loved his speech. Talking slowly, but with emphasis and considerable rhetorical flair, he used his magnificent bass voice to good effect.

"I did not return to Nova Scotia from the arid wastes of Ontario in order to watch the march of progress," he began. "There is quite enough of that to be found west of the Isthmus of Chignecto, creating, I might say, pollution, economic imbalance, labour unrest, and foul working conditions — not to mention a wealth of human greed." He paused and gazed around the audience, eyes steady.

"No!" His voice rose, and the audience started. "I returned to Nova Scotia to reclaim the values that enriched my childhood in this small town. I came back to nourish my old age in an atmosphere of wise and balanced thinking. I settled here in order to find tranquility beside an unravaged sea, to see again the land where beauty and equilibrium prevail."

Mrs. Knickle felt an odd sensation move up and down her spinal column.

Mr. VanBuskirk fixed Mr. Gilbert Hogan with unwavering eyes. "I did not come here in order to see a beautiful park overshadowed by a hideous concrete structure, casting shade on the flowers, discouraging the visitation of wild fowl, filling the air with honking cars, screaming brakes, choking smoke. No! I returned to my native province because I knew — where my confidence was strong — that enlightened attitudes would inhabit the minds of my neighbours. Where I felt that no one would value a dollar more than a flower. Where loveliness and nature would always outweigh the temptations of so-called progress and prosperity."

Someone in the back row yelled out something about jobs and hunger, but he was loudly shushed by the chairman of the meeting. The vote for the factory lost by an enormous margin. Although many people pressed forward to thank Mr. VanBuskirk, he was nowhere to be found. He had chosen a seat near the door, and had slipped out. Mrs. Knickle went home and slept unusually lightly, visited by dreams whose contents were surprising in a lady of seventy-seven years.

Mrs. Knickle now set down her dishcloth and took out a pad. On it she wrote:

Description:
(Assets)
Intelligent
Educated
Confident
Thin

Loves beauty
Hates pollution
Very sexy
Not chatty
Has pension (presumably)
Very desirable
Excellent values
Subtle charisma

It was a daunting list, but Mrs. Knickle was not easily cowed. On the opposite page she wrote:

Strategy:
Lead from strength.

Which was? Find common areas and start there. She cast her eye over the list and decided that she more or less shared all the qualities, with the possible exception of "very sexy" and "not chatty" and "subtle charisma." But opposites often attract. Basil had been tall and exceedingly handsome. Ready to leap into bed at a moment's notice, he had, after all, chosen to leap with her.

"We live ever in hope," said Mrs. Knickle.

A face appeared at the screen door.

"You, too?" it said, and then Ogden walked in, bearing a measuring cup. "My Mom says can we borrow a cup of white sugar?"

"Me too, what?" Mrs. Knickle asked, and then, "No, you can't. I only have brown. White is unhealthy."

"Talk to yourself," Ogden said. "Okay, I'll try Mr. VanBuskirk. I got something to tell him anyways." And he was gone, slamming the door behind him.

❋

On his veranda, Mr. VanBuskirk watched the approach of Ogden and meditated on the youth-of-today. Fancy a child of 1910 daring to suggest to one's betters and one's elders that they talked to themselves. Nevertheless, it was interesting. He wondered if Ogden had consulted his scatterbrained mother — the one who painted those unbridled abstract flower pictures — as to the dangers of talking to oneself. He chuckled deep in his throat and then changed, when Ogden started to climb the steps, to what he hoped was a stern harrumph.

"I need some white sugar for Mom's trifle," Ogden announced, holding out his measuring cup on a straight arm. "It's made of cake and jam and custard. And white sugar. Mrs. Knickle only has brown."

"Very well," Mr. VanBuskirk said, without moving. "However, first I'd like to know if you have approached your good mother on the subject of speaking to oneself."

"Yes," said Ogden. "I have."

"Well?"

"Crazy or old. Sometimes both."

"So! That's the way it is. Old, I can accept. Crazy pleases me less. But one must bow to what the gods decree. Sugar, you say?"

"Yes. White. One cup."

Mr. VanBuskirk rose slowly and took the measuring cup. He entered the house, slamming the screen door behind him. "Crazy and old, eh?" he muttered. Returning with the sugar, he continued, "Damn sight more interesting to converse with myself than with most other people in this two-bit town." He opened the screen door onto the veranda. "Here," he said to

Ogden. "Take your youth and your sanity and your sugar back to your own house."

Ogden grabbed the sugar. "Thanks," he yelled over his shoulder as he leapt down the stairs two at a time, spilling sugar on every step.

Mr. VanBuskirk settled back to his chair and his book, admitting to himself that a little of the glitter had gone out of the day.

✳

Four houses down the street, Mrs. Knickle watched the return of Ogden.

"Get your sugar?" she called down from her veranda.

"Yeah. Old guy talks to himself a lot." He looked at her, sugar trailing out of the tipping cup. "Guess you all do."

Mrs. Knickle frowned. "What I don't understand is who first decided that self-expression was more valuable than manners."

"What? Whatcha say?"

"Nothing. Nothing important. I was just talking to myself."

"My mom says that's a bad sign."

"That's just fine. She is certainly welcome to any diagnosis she may care to make. But I, for one, am not interested in the details. Not in the slightest. Good morning, Ogden."

Ogden went.

"Well," Mrs. Knickle said as she entered the house, closing the door quietly behind her. "Ogden may not be my favourite person, but he has provided me with a significant manoeuvre in my campaign. One must give the devil his due, even when he arrives in Levi's."

The morning was a delightful one — sunny and warm for June, with an invigorating breeze that held a mixture of salt and fish and late lilac. Down by the waterfront could be heard the distant thunk of fish boxes and the intermittent call of male voices. Young Mrs. Ernst was wheeling her newest baby down the sidewalk to the accompanying music of its squeaky wheels. Her three older children trailed behind her, a small parade.

Mrs. Knickle was preparing for her two-mile walk. But today, instead of walking towards the park, she would direct her route past Mr. VanBuskirk's veranda.

Dressed in a pair of grey corduroy pants, a purple sweater, and Birkenstock sandals, Mrs. Knickle set off. Nearing Mr. VanBuskirk's veranda, she slowed. Good. He was there, on his usual chair, reading.

Resolutely, Mrs. Knickle stopped at the foot of his steps and said, "Good morning, Professor VanBuskirk."

Mr. VanBuskirk raised his head, startled. He took off his glasses and rose from his chair.

"Good morning, Miss . . ." he began uncertainly. Third interruption today, he noted darkly.

"Mrs. Knickle," she announced. "Grace Knickle. Forgive me for interrupting you in the middle of your studies, but I just wanted to congratulate you."

Mr. VanBuskirk rallied. It had been quite some time since anyone had congratulated him on anything at all. He had long professed that praise was an unnecessary frill. In fact, he had never been able to understand the late Mrs. VanBuskirk's desire for it. "How do I look?" she would ask anxiously, before they left for a faculty reception. Irritated, he had tended to answer, "Fine. Fine. You always look fine. I would let you know if you didn't." Or she would say, "How was the dinner? Did you like the new recipe?" He had eaten it, hadn't he? Why did Myra need to be forever and ever reinforced? In those days he had felt himself to be impervious to both praise and negative criticism. When his lectures were successful (and they usually were) and the students said so (as they often did), well and good. If the group found him to be dull, to hell with them. It was their loss. The lectures were always full of useful facts. A lecture shouldn't have to be a vaudeville act. If he had wanted to entertain, he could have trained as a comedian.

Mr. VanBuskirk looked at Mrs. Knickle with new interest. Ogden had delivered insanity and senility to him earlier this morning. A compliment — or, as she was saying, congratulations — would be a welcome contrast.

"Whatever for?" he asked, and then, "Won't you sit down?" He pulled up a chair from a corner of the veranda and brushed it off with his pocket handkerchief. Mrs. Knickle mounted the steps and sat.

"On your excellent presentation to the town meeting last month. On your content. And, for that matter . . . " she gazed demurely at her hands in her lap " . . . your delivery. I was very moved."

Mrs. Knickle was surprised by her forwardness. Young girls brought up in the second decade of the twentieth century were taught never to be socially aggressive, especially with gentlemen. And this kind of training dies heard. But she lacked the time for outdated formalities.

"Why, thank you, Mrs. Knickle," Mr. VanBuskirk said, his face serious, his amazing eyes inscrutable.

"The main reason I'm here, however," she went on, "is to say that I'm sorry to have foisted Ogden upon you this morning."

"You foisted Ogden upon me?"

Mrs. Knickle proffered a small smile. "Well, in a manner of speaking. He came to me for white sugar. And I had only brown. It's supposed to be healthier, and at my age, I need all the help I can get." She laughed lightly.

Mr. VanBuskirk looked at Mrs. Knickle's cheerful face and

sprightly movements and felt depressingly old. She must be many years younger than he was. Sixty-six? At most, a youthful sixty-nine.

"Well," he said, suddenly resolving to be honest. "According to Ogden, I need an enormous amount of help. He caught me conversing with the ether. Told me that talking to myself was an ominous sign. I was unwise enough to ask him to elucidate."

"And?"

"It seems I am either crazy or old. Or both."

"If so," announced Mrs. Knickle jubilantly, "then there are two crazy people on the block."

And presumably old, too. Mr. VanBuskirk's spirits rose.

"I've been talking to myself," she continued, "ever since I learned to speak, at eleven months."

Mr. VanBuskirk sighed. Oh, well. Bright, apparently. But young. All that energy.

"Now then," Mrs. Knickle said, "I must be off for my daily walk. Oh . . . How did you enjoy the Liberal convention last night? It seemed to me that the wrong man won, and for all the wrong reasons." She waited expectantly, standing.

"I'm a Conservative, myself," he said. "Couldn't care less who wins in that godforsaken party. Who did?"

Mrs. Knickle was thunderstruck, and didn't answer. Clearly, political science was not his field. But one expects a certain awareness, a certain concern about matters national and political, no matter what the academic discipline.

"Would you enjoy a lemonade?" Mr. VanBuskirk asked suddenly. "It could help you on your walk. Give you strength, perhaps."

Mrs. Knickle sat down again. "That would be simply lovely," she said, and looked quietly out at the street as he rose from his seat. Mrs. Ernst was still trailing up and down, up and down the street with her brood; the lilac bush on Mr. VanBuskirk's lawn was at its prime; a butterfly went loping by in the warm air.

Bang! Mr. VanBuskirk slammed the screen door even harder than Ogden as he entered the house. Mrs. Knickle winced, but did so philosophically. One must not expect perfection.

After what seemed to Mrs. Knickle a very long time, Mr. VanBuskirk returned, bearing a tray with two glasses, two napkins, and a plate of dry crackers.

"Sorry," he said. "No cookies or cake. Ogden said his mother needed the sugar for a trifle. I almost said, 'I'll give you a cup of sugar only on the condition that you bring me a dish of trifle for my supper.' But instead, I listened to his insults and let him go, unchallenged. Haven't seen a homemade cookie since Myra died twelve years ago." He wondered vaguely if he was hinting, and hoped not.

Mrs. Knickle was just tucking this bit of information into her mental pocket when a swallow flew into the veranda and lit on a shelf under the eaves.

"Shoo! Shoo!" Mr. VanBuskirk was suddenly awkwardly active, clapping his hands, stomping around the veranda. "That confounded bird has been dickering for a roost on that shelf all week. With any encouragement she'll make a nest and have a whole flock of open-mouthed babies. Then try to read your book in peace. Fat chance. Can't stand birds. Goddamn fluttery things."

A deep sadness settled on Mrs. Knickle's heart. A Conservative, and an ignorant Conservative at that. A door slammer. A hater of birds, and apparently of young things in general. What on earth kind of professor had he been, anyway?

Mrs. Knickle sipped her lemonade. "May I ask you what subject you taught before you retired, Professor VanBuskirk?"

She wondered if he didn't like people interrupting his reading, either. But she was really thinking about Christmas, and about Mary's children running around making a noise. She could visualize Mr. VanBuskirk retiring to his study (created from the old playroom in the basement), scowling. She had been going to suggest that he might like to accompany her on her walk. But after watching his slow progress from his rocker to the door, and from the door to her chair, she changed her mind. Too slow. He'd never be able to match her pace. Probably be a slow dish dryer, too — if he ever deigned to dry dishes at all.

"Physics," he replied. "The book I'm reading right now is on the quantum theory. Old, but forever new. Was, is, and always will be. The book's a bit old hat, but still intriguing."

"My majors in university were history and English," Mrs. Knickle ventured. "I felt that in studying those two subjects I could come closest to understanding life. One discipline tells it as it really was, the other as the imagination perceives it — which can be even more valid." She had rehearsed this speech this morning, before leaving the house.

"Physics is my life," he continued, starting his sentence before she had quite finished hers. "To me, it is my contact with Cosmos; it is my private denial of Chaos. Mathematics is the great ordering force. Just think! The entire universe, galaxy upon galaxy, moves in accordance with its laws!" His eyes were alive now, sparked by some source of power that Mrs. Knickle would never understand.

"Myself," she pressed on, "I feel that people are the key to the part of the universe that matters. Simple everyday experiences, culminating in pain or love. These are the things that are of concern to me." Galaxies be darned, she thought.

He did not answer. His gaze was on the lilac bush, but his

thoughts were elsewhere. Embracing the quantum theory, she supposed.

Abruptly she got up to leave. "Thank you so much, Professor VanBuskirk, for the lemonade and cracker. Fuel for my walk. And don't worry about talking to yourself. I've been doing it for seventy-five and one-half years."

And started at eleven months. It did not take Mr. VanBuskirk long to do this piece of arithmetic. She was seventy-seven years old. Stunned, he did not even say goodbye. He just raised his hand in a gesture of farewell.

Mrs. Knickle's walk was not a success. She felt tired and moved more slowly than usual. She developed a blister on her right heel and had to stop at Lawton's Drug Store for Band-Aids, lest the blister burst and stain her expensive sandals. She met Ogden later on and he asked, "What's the matter?" What did he mean, *"What's the matter?"* A person must look pretty terrible before someone, even Ogden, asks "What's the matter?" Ogden was standing beside the town duck pond at the time. She thought about how pleasurable it would be to push him right into the water, to watch him glurp and splutter. She pictured herself standing there, dry, complacent, saying to the sodden figure, "What's the matter, Ogden?" She smiled sadly as she walked on.

Well, it had been a nice idea. She had assumed that any man with a Ph.D. and a flat stomach, a man who could make that inspiring speech to the town meeting, must be a lively and stimulating person, in tune with her own sensitivities, alive to the issues of the day. She had taken it for granted that he would not slam doors, although she had to grin at her own naïveté.

She had always placed professors on pedestals, but surely by now she must be old enough to know better. Professor Gibson, that sweet-syllabled orator who had taught her Romantic poetry at university, was said to have beaten his children with a razor strap when they failed to wash their hands before dinner. And Professor O'Flaherty. He of the beautiful smile and the musical accent, who taught moral philosophy every Monday and Wednesday at 10:30 a.m., had actually placed his hand on her thigh one morning after class, when he was discussing her essay topic with her. And *squeezed* it. She had never forgotten it, and henceforth it was as though her thigh were tainted. Squeeze anything else, she had often thought, later in life, but keep your hands off my right thigh. It had always puzzled Basil — and small wonder. "What on earth is so special about that leg?" he'd say, irritated, when she would cringe from his touch. And every time she saw that meek little wife of Professor O'Flaherty's downtown or at a concert she would actually feel again that outrageous pressure.

However, it now appeared to Mrs. Knickle that she was to spend the rest of her life without squeezing of any kind. As she walked through Centennial Gardens she watched the strolling couples and felt a wave of deep regret. Old age might change you on the outside. But inside you felt exactly the same as when you were young. She ached with envy of the young people around her. Mr. VanBuskirk had seemed such a perfect solution to her loneliness. She walked home so slowly that there could not possibly have been any cardiovascular benefit whatsoever.

But Mrs. Knickle was already switching her channel by the time she arrived home. She entered the house, closing the screen door carefully, quietly, behind her. She was tired. How lovely to be able to sit down before the soaps with a peanut butter sandwich, instead of having to prepare a complicated lunch for someone else. How nice to be able to indulge her interest in *The Young and the Restless* without worrying about the almost-certain disapproval of a higher mind — a mind fixed on galaxies.

"Hello, Jonas dear," she said to her canary, admiring his plumage and his voice. Observing the dustballs skittering across the floor, she thought aloud, "Go ahead. Skitter. I'm in no mood today to deal with you." Then she ate her sandwich, watched her program, and went to bed, sleeping soundly for exactly forty-five minutes.

When she awoke, the beautiful sunny day had deteriorated and dark clouds were gathering in the west and overhead. An intermittent plink-plink on the rain spouting told her what she could expect for the rest of the day. A few stray gulls flew across the sky swiftly, purposefully, without their usual lazy gyrations. A storm, she knew, was on its way. And a good one. "There will be wind, and a lot of rain," she said. "Which calls for a fire in the grate and a book on the sofa." She changed into her purple housecoat, the one with the embroidered yoke and the covered buttons, gift of her youngest son on her most recent birthday. Then she lit the fire and settled herself on the sofa with an afghan, a glass of dry sherry, and one of Robertson Davies' novels.

"It's a sign," she said, contentedly. "It was meant to be. The storm came in order to remind me of this fact." She hugged her freedom close to herself and smiled quietly. That was at 2:30.

At 3:30, two logs and fifty-nine pages later, the doorbell rang. Mrs. Knickle left her comfortable nest on the sofa, and placed her book, open and butter-side down, on the afghan. She could see through the window that the rain was descending in driving, gusting curtains of grey. She opened the front door.

It was Mr. VanBuskirk. Without umbrella or raincoat, he stood there, unbelievably wet, a measuring cup in his hand.

"I beg your pardon," he said. "I'm dripping all over your

carpet," for she had gestured that he come in from the veranda. The wind was such that the rain reached right across into the front door. And it was cold. She closed the door and tried to bring her astonishment under control.

"It never occurred to me that one could get this wet, going just the distance of four houses," Mr. VanBuskirk said, water running into his eyes and dripping into his collar.

It crossed Mrs. Knickle's mind that anyone with an advanced knowledge of physics could have figured this out. "Here," she said briskly, suddenly all efficiency. "Come in by the fire. Take off your shirt and wrap yourself in that afghan. I'll get one of Basil's old sweaters for you. Unless, of course, you want to get pneumonia and spoil the entire summer for yourself. Sit down on that wingback chair."

When she returned with Basil's sweater — a soft red cashmere that she could never bring herself to dispose of — Mr. VanBuskirk was sitting huddled in the chair, engulfed by the afghan.

"I think I'm getting your chair wet," he shivered. He reflected for a moment. Myra would not have liked that at all, and would have rushed to get newspapers or cushions to put under him.

"Don't talk nonsense," Mrs. Knickle said brusquely. "Here's a towel to dry yourself, and a sweater. Put it on while I'm making coffee. Would you like it laced with a little whisky to warm you up?"

Mr. VanBuskirk turned his amazing eyes upon her, and said simply, "Oh my!"

She gave him ten minutes to recover his temperature and his dignity, and then returned with two steaming cups of Irish coffee and a plate of lemon-frosted carrot cake.

"Don't talk," she said. "Just eat. You'll feel better in a minute."

He did. He felt better almost immediately. His shaggy grey hair had been towelled vigorously and was already starting to dry. He smiled shyly above his whisky-coffee.

"I came to borrow some brown sugar," he said, his eyes avoiding hers. "I like it on my porridge. Oatmeal. I knew you had some. Because of Ogden, you know."

"Yes," she said. She did not say that it seemed an odd day to choose to collect it.

Mr. VanBuskirk looked up from his coffee. "I see you have a canary," he said. "As birds go, it's attractive. Although I feel that wild things should be free. However, it sings nicely. I don't think it would disturb a person who was reading." Then he added gloomily, "I keep a cat."

She absorbed this extraordinary paragraph. "Yes, I know," she said. "So do I."

"Yes? Oh. Well, well. It doesn't endanger the canary?"

"I have yet to see the cat that can climb a stainless steel rod. And the canary, as you so aptly pointed out, is not free."

"Yes. Yes, of course."

There was a silence that was not uncomfortable.

"I've read your book." He nodded towards the volume on the sofa. "I found the ending very contrived."

Mrs. Knickle spoke carefully. "So far, I like it a lot," she said. "I'll assess the ending when I get there."

"Your cake," he said slowly — everything he did seemed to be slow — "is like an edible poem."

"Or perhaps like edible physics."

He chuckled. "More like physics. Because physics is beyond poetry, and better."

And then there followed a lively discussion, an out-and-out argument on poetry versus physics. She knew again that delicious sensation of mental tautness which she had almost

forgotten. That lively reaching for the logical reply. That rally-
ing of ideas, like an invigorating game of tennis. When they had
finished their discussion, no opinions had changed. But it had
been fun. It had been stimulating to feel that brisk turning of
cerebral wheels.

At five o'clock, Mr. VanBuskirk rose slowly from the wingback chair. "I see the storm is over," he said. "I must be going.
Supper, you know."

Mrs. Knickle resisted the temptation to ask him to share the
remains of last night's casserole. She didn't want to proceed
with undue haste. Besides, a gourmet cook doesn't want to
make her debut with a menu of leftovers.

"Oh!" she said suddenly, as he reached the door. "I forgot."
She hurried back to the kitchen.

"Here," she said. "Your sugar. I'm getting so forgetful. And
a bit of carrot cake for your supper."

Mr. VanBuskirk looked gratefully at Mrs. Knickle. He observed her crazy hairdo, the profusion of white curls. He
admired her bright eyes. He marvelled at her quick movements. He coughed slightly.

"Mrs. Knickle," he began. This was difficult for him. He
could not draw on a lifetime of habit. "Mrs. Knickle. I would
like to tell you that I like your . . . robe. A very lovely colour.
And becoming. And I thank you for your rescue mission."

He watched her. His compliment had pleased her. It was
clear to him that this was so. The delight in her eyes was
unmistakable. He sighed as he turned towards the porch. Poor
Myra. It would have been so easy. He opened the screen door
and slammed it behind him.

Mrs. Knickle scarcely heard the slamming of the door. She
did not move out to the kitchen to preheat the oven. Instead,
she went into the living room and sat down on a footstool,

staring at the fire. She was a little bit sad. It was that remark about the purple housecoat that had done it. With one blow, he had deprived her of her freedom — acquired, relinquished, and freshly regained. She knew he would never speed up. Clearly there was slowness built right into his genes. That screen door would be slamming until she died. Two cats in one house argue over territory — just like two people. Jonas would be safe, but possibly too nervous to sing. Mr. VanBuskirk was unlikely to be the type to dry dishes, either quickly or slowly.

Then she rose from the footstool and looked at herself in the mirror above the mantelpiece. She passed her right hand across the embroidered yoke of her housecoat, and down the soft purple material of her left sleeve. She smiled to herself in the glass. "Becoming," she whispered.

"Nothing," she said aloud, as she went out to the kitchen to heat her tuna casserole, "is ever simple."

ELLIOT'S DAUGHTER

May 3

I have decided to keep a journal. Not a diary, exactly. An account of sorts — of my life and certain of my thoughts.

I am a writer — or so I like to call myself. Some writers refer to themselves as authors, but this is a pretentious term, and very few writers use it. Amateurs very frequently call themselves authors, but this is an almost sure sign of their inferior status. But I do not look upon myself as an amateur, in spite of the fact that my work has seldom been published — three times, if I must be absolutely honest: one short story in a South Shore contest (first prize), one article on the care and feeding of cats, and a poem entitled "Litany," which, to my great astonishment and delight, was accepted five years ago by an Upper Canadian literary magazine. It was this last triumph which I felt pushed me out of the amateur status and into the heady world of professionalism. After all, those literary journals are usually juried by English professors and established writers.

"Litany" was written in free verse — my first attempt at this form, or lack of it. Usually I am more at home with a regular meter and a predictable rhyme scheme. I am by nature an orderly and somewhat contained man (I almost said gentleman, but I realize that this word — in fact, this concept — is very much out of date), but I took considerable satisfaction from the fact that the words and the lines of my poem wandered (I was about to say jumped) all over the page, with a freedom that I would at one time have regarded as licentious. I'm sure I don't know what came over me that day. That night, actually. I do remember that I awakened in the middle of the night after a dream whose contents I could not or would not identify. All I recall is that I woke up in the grip of a terrible rage. Sleep was impossible — or maybe I was afraid to return to it — so I turned on the bed lamp and began to write. I let my fury carry me along (there was no possibility of recollecting anything in tranquility that night) and the result was truly extraordinary. When I reread it in the morning, I could scarcely believe that it was I who had written it. It wasn't just the form that was out of character — all those staggering lines and dancing words. The content was bizarre also. It was full of profanity and a great deal of unbridled sex. I could only dimly remember having written it. It was like the memory of some fevered fantasy that occurs during a grave illness.

But even in the cold dawn of the next day. I was able to see that the poem was good. I could not honestly recognize what it meant, what the poet (I) was communicating. But I sensed a kind of profundity lurking somewhere within or between the lines. Consciously hurrying lest I change my mind, I scrabbled around in my desk until I found a suitable envelope. Then I typed out the poem — with all its strange pauses and detours intact — wrote a brief covering letter, and addressed it to the editor of a quite prestigious university journal, complete with SASE. You see? In spite of my less-than-spectacular publishing record, I know the proper procedure, as well as the correct terminology that goes along with it. Self-Addressed Stamped Envelope. For rejections, about which I know a great deal.

And that is not all about which I am knowledgeable. Always a clean copy. Generous margins. Page numbers in the top right-hand corner. No staples. And so on.

May 6

Let me tell you a bit about myself. I have said *you,* because when one writes in a diary or a journal one certainly has a sense of speaking to someone. Not to oneself, and not to any real person. But undeniably a person, perhaps a mythical one. But to continue: I am unmarried, forty-three years of age, a postal clerk. Because I work in a small substation of the postal system, I have become familiar with some of the people who live in that area of the city. One of these people is a writer. His name is Elliot Archer. I'm sure you will have heard of him. He writes novels, the occasional excellent short story, sometimes a poem. I follow his career with great interest, for obvious reasons. Profiles of his life and work appear in local and national newspapers. Even Peter Gzowski has seen fit to interview him. He actually supports himself on his writing. He has no other job. This is practically unheard of in the writing world, and impresses me deeply. Almost all of us must have other forms of employment if we are to avoid starvation. Not he. He lives simply — I have searched out his home and inspected it, assessing its worth, envying him his independence and his success. His house is small and would benefit from a coat of paint. It is in an undistinguished part of the city. But he owns it (I've checked on that, also), and it is free of any debilitating mortgage.

Elliot Archer is also not dying of hunger, for I have seen him myself in the local supermarket, his cart as full of food as anyone else's. I always take note of what he buys, and certain items keep reappearing with an intriguing regularity. He has a chronic fondness for Sara Lee chocolate cakes, ripple potato chips, black olives, Oreo cookies, and tonic water. It is a rare day, indeed, when one sees a head of lettuce or a good red tomato in his cart. He is fat and puffy looking, and his colour is not good. I also have to say that he often appears ill-tempered — or possibly just plagued by anxiety.

Anxiety. I find myself asking, as I follow him from frozen foods to baked goods to dairy products (of which he buys very little), why or how can such a man be anxious? I watch those Priority Post items come sailing in for him week after week, with the names of this publisher and that celebrity written on their backs. Proofs? Essential correspondence? Notices of grants or awards or foreign sales? I would be frozen with shock were I to receive a parcel or letter by way of Priority Post. But he picks them up, heavy-lidded with boredom (or tiredness, maybe — I must be fair), looks casually at the back to verify the sender, mutters his thanks, and bumbles off towards the entrance. To home, then, to read his important mail over a gin and tonic or a Sara Lee cake. While I remain behind my counter, stripping off stamps, writing money orders, taking out my frustrations with the thump of the date stamp. It makes me angry that he does not seem more pleased to be Elliot Archer.

May 10
Let me speak a bit more about Elliot. (I've come to call him by his first name in the privacy of my own mind.) I don't know

whether or not he is married. The interviews mention his career but not his domestic arrangements. But he is always alone when I see him. Either his wife is an invalid, stuffed away like Rochester's crazed spouse in some back room of his little house, or she is dead, or else perhaps he has chosen to remain single. Like me.

But that is not entirely accurate. I have not exactly chosen to remain a bachelor. I am full of fantasies which endow me with literary successes and a plethora of Priority Post envelopes. But certainly another of my fantasies includes a cozy house (with six-over-six windows, shutters, a small neat garden) and a warm and loving wife (a pretty, smiling face in the doorway, the smell of muffins reaching me before I even open the gate, someone to whom I can read my first drafts). But obtaining that pretty and smiling wife has not proved to be an easy matter.

I am not handsome, nor have I ever been what one would call attractive. Or so I was led to believe by my father. And by my brother, Victor, whose physical and intellectual perfections were my own personal trial by fire during the eighteen long years when we inhabited the same house. I will admit, in the privacy of this journal, that it is not easy to be related to someone who does almost nothing wrong — except, of course, taunting and belittling his little brother, which were his two favourite and secret flaws. But quite apart from that, how can you compete with someone who comes first in every exam, who is captain of the school hockey team, who is equipped with broad shoulders (as early as the age of ten), smouldering eyes, and a shock of unruly black hair. I am of medium height, medium colouring, medium intelligence, medium athletic ability. If I robbed a bank at the height of noon without a mask and ran off with a bagful of money, the police would never find me. I look like too many other people — bland, featureless, even lacking the distinction of compelling ugliness, like Elliot Archer's. He looks a bit like a distinguished rhinoceros — bumbling and gross, but with a face and form that one would never, under any circumstances, forget.

It has been my misfortune in life to envy a lot of people — my brother, all members of the school hockey team, movie stars, those who excel at Trivial Pursuit, all published writers. When my father first told me that I was just about as distinguished as a jellyfish (and then punched me jovially and laughed, apparently surprised that I was not more amused), I believed what he said. "Gotta be able to take a joke, son," he'd say, every time he introduced the jellyfish theme — which was often. A jellyfish — if you've never seen one — is flat and colourless, moves in an indeterminate way that suggests a deficiency of purpose or direction, and lacks a spine. On the frequent occasions when I was likened to a jellyfish, I would grind my teeth (which I visualized as being worn down to flat nubbins, all twenty-eight of them) and tell myself that a common jellyfish is closely related to a Portuguese man-of-war; it simply lacks the colour and the long poisonous stingers. But even as I thought this, I knew that the differences were more significant than the similarities. A jellyfish just sort of galumphs through the water. A man-of-war, with its long, rhythmically swaying streamers, is a floating menace, possessed of a strange and dangerous beauty.

My mother? A gentle and ineffectual woman, who deplored the way I was put down by my father, but who did nothing to prevent it. But, to be fair to that long-suffering lady, I will say that on the rare occasions when she limped to my defence, the fallout was more painful and probably more damaging to me than its original source. Father's rage was fierce at such times. She was turning the boy against him. She was a wimp, herself, and to hell with her opinion. How could she expect the boy to develop backbone if she rushed to protect him from the perfectly normal give-and-take of daily life? It crossed my mind that it was he that was doing the giving, while I was in perpetual charge of the taking. But of course I said nothing. He had high blood pressure, and we were supposed to keep this in mind.

These journal conversations are long ones. It occurs to me that I may be writing a diary in order to avoid writing anything else.

May 11

I see that yesterday's entry was intended to be a commentary on my marital state. But I was sidetracked by domestic confessions. A discussion of family frailties is a hard subject to leave.

I cannot remember a time when I liked Victor. I suppose this means that he started his attacks upon me very early. No doubt he pinched me as I lay in my baby carriage. He would have enjoyed that. But the memory of things he did — small things, maybe even unintentional things — still has the power to hurt me at the age of forty-three. I recall making a lawn ornament. I had laboriously cut out the form from a discarded piece of wood, and painted the result. I thought it was a thing of wonder, and asked my mother if I might stick it in the lawn. Yes, I could. She told me it was lovely. I was beside myself with pride and deep contentment. After my brother saw it, he retired to the basement, remaining down there for five hours. It was a Saturday, and it was raining. On Sunday, the smell of fresh paint wafted up to the main floor. Innocent fool that I was, I had no idea what he was doing. On Monday morning, there they were, apparently put out the night before — three more lawn ornaments, perfectly cut, perfectly painted, perfectly placed.

I left the house that morning with my father and Victor. "Aha!" exclaimed my father, his face alive with smiles. "That's the way to do it!" Then he stopped in front of my ornament, threw back his head, and roared with laughter. When he finished with his awful mirth, he turned to me and said, "Well, it's important to try." He patted me vaguely on the head. To Victor he said, "Good work, my son!"

That afternoon, when no one was at home, I went out to the front lawn and savagely pulled my ornament out of the ground. Wrapping it in a brown paper bag, I walked the half mile down to the harbour, and threw it into the sea.

Eventually, Victor dealt me the bitterest blow that he could possibly have devised. He died. At the age of eighteen, in the prime of his young manhood — tall, athletic, pursued by more young women than he could possibly accommodate, headed for law school, adored by his parents — he contracted meningitis, and was dead within a week.

My parents' grief was so absolute that I felt annihilated by it. In that one week, they lost both of their sons, although they were not aware of this at the time. My brother's perfection was now embalmed. From now on, my father would compare me with Victor with even less mercy. Placed beside his dreams of what my brother might have become was the reality of what I was. I would remain forever the jellyfish to Victor's man-of-war. I would never, ever, as long as I lived, be able to surpass my brother in anything at all. His death deprived me of this, and I hated him for it.

Picture me, then, at the age of sixteen, destined to be second-rate for the rest of my life. But ultimately a wife would have helped. Or even, when still young, just an adoring girlfriend. But adoring girls did not surround me like swarming flies, as they had done to Victor. I was attracted to the wrong girls — to the school stars, the cheerleaders, the bright and flashy ones. My advances to them were shy and uncertain, and no one flew into my arms. Looking back now, I think they probably didn't even know I was advancing. "Not much of a stud," said my father. "Not like Victor."

May 29

I have learned that Elliot Archer is — or was — a married man. Today he came to the postal station to buy an Express Post envelope. "For Geraldine," he said, turning to a friend in the line-up. "I have to let her know if I have room for her. She'd like to come in on the Monday train. Just a short visit. To lick her wounds."

Geraldine? I tried to keep my mind on the ripping of stamps and the making of change, without impeding my efforts to hear everything. *Licking her wounds?*

"What a helluva month for a daughter to choose to come visiting!"

A daughter! The man was unjustly blessed — not only with a successful writing career, but with a daughter as well.

"That will be $6.41 with the GST," I said to my customer, as Elliot talked on.

"If she can't keep her marriage intact, she needn't think that she can come crawling back into the nest. He wasn't *my* choice. And she says she'll be here for twelve days. Wants to be out of town while some legal wrangling is taking place. Goddamn time to pick! Revisions due on one book in three weeks, and the proofs of my other one arriving in the next couple of days. Couldn't be a worse time for me to have to act like a father." He muttered something under his breath and heaved an enormous

sigh. "She can come, but I absolutely refuse to have my concen-
tration interfered with." He stepped up to the counter as my
other customer moved away.

"One Express Post envelope," he said. "And twenty regular
stamps."

I swallowed. "You'd be more sure of it arriving quickly if
you sent it by Priority Post," I offered.

He looked at me sharply. "Too bloody expensive," he
growled. He turned to his friend. "Express Post will probably
get it to Toronto on time, and if it doesn't, it's not my problem.
Hasn't she ever heard of the telephone?"

And haven't *you*? I countered, but not, of course, aloud.

Tonight I have but one wish. That it be necessary for Geraldine to put something into the mail when she comes for a visit.
I want to see what Elliot has produced in the way of a child.
Something cranky and swarthy, I expect. Egotistical and assert-
ive. But on the other hand, anyone who rushes for refuge to a
man like Elliot must be in a pretty desolate condition.

June 4

My complaints to you have been mainly about my father and
my brother. But it was really my mother who kept me from
marrying. She unmercifully criticized the only two girls I
brought home for her approval. "Not good enough for you,"
she declared, clinging to her one remaining child, in spite of his
inadequacies. Also, I think she was taking this opportunity to
assert herself in a significant way, in an area where she could
actually exercise some control. I can forgive her for this,
because I'm able to see that she must have been starved almost
to death with a hunger to control something or somebody.
Maybe I didn't recognize — at that time — all the facets of her
disapproval of those two girls. Sometimes I don't even really

know what is going on in my own head until I write it all down. Anyway, for whatever reason — habit, maybe — fear, perhaps — I listened to her, both times. And I acquiesced.

Not until I was thirty-five years old did I leave home. No doubt you find that difficult to believe. Every time I would announce my intention to leave, my mother would burst into tears and sob, "Don't leave me! Don't leave me!" I knew perfectly well what she meant by that. She meant: "Don't leave me alone with your father." What does a jellyfish do when a current is running so strongly in one direction? But two weeks after my mother died, I moved from Victoria to Halifax, putting an entire continent between my father and me.

June 7

I saw Geraldine today. She was in the grocery store with her father. She has a small tidy face, large brown eyes, and absolutely straight light-brown hair. Beside Elliot, she looked beige all over. Although he was dressed in black, the colour that came to mind was red. He looked that intense. Thinking about his proofs, I thought, my heart squeezed with envy. Proofs should be a cause for great joy. Proofs mean that a book is on its way. Unbeetle your brow, I demanded. Your daughter is with you. Your book is coming.

Geraldine looked full of anxiety. If you were desperate enough to flee to Elliot Archer for comfort, I thought, what on earth kind of trauma did you leave behind? Maybe tomorrow you will need some stamps.

June 9

Today she came and bought a small package of stamped envelopes. I smiled at her as I handed her the change. Timidly, sadly, she smiled back. A warm light softened and brightened her tight little face. I felt something inside me lurch convulsively. This girl was not the kind who usually attracted me. No colour. No flash. She was very small. Why was I finding it necessary to lean against the counter and to breathe deeply?

Her name is Geraldine, I mused. Elliot would have preferred a son, and would have named him Gerald. Why could he not have named her Sylvia or Anne or Madeline? Why did he have to enshrine his preference in her name, for all to see?

"Thank you," she said, and left. Her voice was husky and very gentle.

June 11
Last night I couldn't sleep, so eventually I decided to make use of my insomnia instead of fighting it. At 3:15 a.m., I shuffled over to my desk, pulled my paper and pen from the drawer, and started to write. I was very, very tired by the time I began, and my usual constraints were abandoned. I felt exhausted, dispirited, reckless. In that state of mind, I wrote a love poem — for whom and to whom, I did not bother to inquire. I just wrote it. After a brief sleep, I rose at seven a.m., showered, shaved, and reread the poem. It was very good. The subject of the poem was quite clearly Geraldine.

Today she didn't come into the post office. Elliot has said she would be home for twelve days. Hastily I counted off the days on my fingers. Six down and six to go. Not much time. I feel something akin to panic.

June 13
I'm not sleeping much at all this week. The long nights are spent in an angry replay of my past, and in a dispirited contemplation of my future. I have read that a mentally healthy person has an eager and positive attitude towards the present. But, try as I

will, I cannot see that the present has much to offer me. I try all the gimmicks and ploys suggested by Sunday school and the *Reader's Digest*. I address myself sternly: Think positively. You are not hungry. You do not live in a war-torn zone. You are not a paraplegic. You dwell in a beautiful city of treelined streets and charming old houses, surrounded on three sides by views of the sea. Although your father left bruises on your spirit, he left none on your body. It is almost summertime, and the air is very soft. You are a writer, and you have just written an excellent poem. You have reason to rejoice.

But rejoice I cannot. This is Day 8, and Geraldine has not reappeared. I have done what I can to make this happen. I have searched the mailbags for Express Post envelopes and Priority Post items, which I would be quite prepared to deliver by hand, in spite of the irregularities of such a move. I've travelled up and down Elliot's street several times, exercising Mrs. Harvey's golden retriever in order to give a certain legitimacy to this unaccustomed walking to and fro. I've spent an inordinate amount of time in the supermarket, knowing that although a person can live ten days without stamps, the need for food is a different matter altogether. But Geraldine probably does the grocery shopping while I'm at work. Once this week I saw Elliot. He was lumbering through the streets, hands clasped behind his back, head down. And mumbling. No doubt he was composing.

If I see her, I will do something. I don't yet know what I will do. But it will be something. I think of those girls in high school who didn't even know I was pursuing them when I made my shy advances. I am determined that this will not happen again. I am forty-three. I will not ever be young again, and I am marching slowly but unavoidably in the direction of fifty. I am feeling a fear of something that is even more compelling than my shyness. Yes, if given the opportunity, I will certainly do something.

In the meantime, in the brief intervals between stamps and registrations and money orders, I think about Geraldine's startlingly clean, shoulder-length, light-brown, straight, beautiful hair. I want to touch it, and I know that it will be warm and slippery in its fineness. She looks to be about thirty-five. Not too late to bear a child. I am pleased that we look enough alike to be sister and brother. The child will resemble both of us. I can feel myself smiling tenderly as I put yet another parcel on the scales. "Will this be regular or expedited mail?" I say to the man who handed it to me, regarding this stranger with real affection. I can see that a heavy rain is falling. I think about how beautiful it looks, and I admire the wet faces of my customers as they approach the counter.

June 14

I saw her again today. I saw Geraldine. She was wandering about the drugstore in which my postal station is located. In spite of all my resolutions to act decisively should she reappear, I was powerless to do a single thing. I was trapped behind my counter — one-half hour before my scheduled coffee break — with a long line-up of customers facing me. But their needs were uncomplicated — no registered letters, no parcels for Hong Kong — and I was free to watch her. She moved up and down the aisles, gazing at displays of Band-Aids, cold remedies, baby powder, vitamins, greeting cards. But she touched nothing, bought nothing. Killing time, I thought, as I weighed a small package. Then she stopped before a display of bubble bath concoctions, picking one bottle off the shelf, inspecting the label, checking the price, putting it back. Too expensive? Too self-indulgent a substance to pour into a bathtub owned by Elliot Archer? She touched the bottle again — almost tenderly, I felt — before walking away. I visualized her immersed in a thick cloud of bubbles, one small firm breast partly visible, her eyes closed.

She must have sensed that I was watching her. Slowly, she looked up and met my eyes. Then she smiled and raised her right hand in a tentative half-wave. Clutching a two-dollar bill, I held up my own hand.

My customer coughed, and I handed him his change.

I want to order a whole case of that bubble bath and leave it on Elliot's veranda.

June 15
Not a good day. No sign, no sight of Geraldine.

June 16
Where can she be? I patrol the neighbourhood during my lunch hour and after five. I buy groceries twice daily. I walk Mrs. Harvey's dog. All to no avail. Maybe she left sooner than she planned.

June 17
I saw her from afar today. She was sitting on a bench in the Public Gardens, hands clasped in her lap, looking straight ahead, her huge eyes like stones. I had brought my sandwich over at noontime, to eat beside the duck pond. It was Day 12, and I had hoped that I might be cheered up by the swans, the flowers, the muddy little lake, even the pigeons.

When I saw her, I reacted exactly as I would have done at sixteen or seventeen. My legs felt as though they no longer belonged to me, and my breathing was painful and short. I held on to the back of a park bench in order to steady myself and to plan my strategy. For she was alone. A merciful Providence had delivered unto me this miracle.

But no. It appeared that Providence had done no such thing. Coming along the path from the canteen was Elliot, stomping along between the flower beds, armed with two ice cream cones, one large, one small. I sat down on the bench and watched them, systematically feeding my entire lunch to the muttering pigeons.

Elliot handed her the small ice cream, and began to pace up and down in front of the bench, gesticulating angrily. I couldn't hear what he was saying, but the tone was unmistakable. He pointed at her, at the sky, at himself, and clenched his fat fist. He took frequent bites of his large ice cream, cramming it into his mouth and then talking with his mouth full. Geraldine sat in exactly the same position as before, except that she held the ice cream in both hands, not eating it. Gradually it started to melt, and although it began to run down between her fingers, she paid no attention to it.

My mind was full of urgent fantasies. I felt that her chest must be close to suffocation, pressured by a high-pitched unexpressed howl. She must want to kill him, I insisted, to claw at his eyes, to draw blood. In that moment, I felt I understood everything there was to know about hate, and possibly about murder.

Another concept presented itself to me, and I was stunned by the force of its clarity. She loves him. She probably hates him, but she loves him, too. I thought about my own father, and realized that most of my pain derived not from the rage I had felt but from the unreturned love that was rotting away in my heart. I could hardly bear to look at the corollary to that discovery — that possibly many or most of the children who suffer at the hands of their parents love them, somewhere deep down beneath the brittle surface of their hatred. The whipped, the abandoned, the sexually abused, the insulted, the neglected, the ridiculed — they all want, most of all, for their parents to appear in the doorway and say, "I love you. I honour you. You are of value to me." And best of all: "I'm sorry." And if that happened, what an avalanche of forgiveness would be let loose upon the world.

The outrageous injustice of such a quick and easy forgiveness stabbed me. A fresh and unfamiliar kind of anger possessed me.

Even as I reacted to those thoughts, Geraldine rose from the bench, neck stiff, hands dripping, and walked slowly towards the large wrought-iron garden gates. Her ice cream lay on the path, attacked by pigeons; her father, at last speechless, was staring after her, his face angry and desolate.

I wrote a poem when I returned home this evening. I called it "Love and Hate," but it lacked what literary critics used to call decorum. I think I know what I want to say, but it will take awhile — some recollection perhaps, some tranquility — before I can convert that raw emotion into something that contains more art than therapy.

June 19

Elliot seems to be writing letters again, because today he has twice visited the post office. My own writing is not going well. I am very depressed.

July 4

It is now Day 17. I think of each day now in terms of how much time has gone by since Geraldine left. I may stop writing this journal. I seem to have learned from it nothing at all.

July 5

Nothing at all.

July 6

This has been a difficult day for me. I thought I saw Geraldine. I was *sure* I saw her. I was cashing a cheque at the Bank of Nova Scotia on Spring Garden Road when I looked out the window and saw a small person disappear around the corner. Same size, same sleek brown hair, same carriage, the same way of moving. Or so — for one electric instant — I thought. Then sanity returned, and I reminded myself that she has been back in Toronto for nineteen long days. I could feel myself blushing as I accepted my money from the cashier.

July 7

I miss the satisfaction and the release of writing about my memories and my thoughts. But at the moment I seem to have only one thought worth expressing. And giving voice to it gives me no release, no satisfaction.

July 13

Today Elliot approached my counter in the company of one of his friends. I have often felt that this man should have no friends whatsoever. He is undeserving of such blessings. But we must not waste our energies groping for evidences of justice in this life. Besides, Elliot has many faces, many masks. I have observed this. He smiles affably at his friends. He dredges up humour from heaven knows what secret places in his mind. His jokes are funny. I have sometimes felt in danger of laughing.

Listen to this: I heard him say, "I don't know why she didn't return to Toronto. When she's that far away, I seldom think about her. Goddamnit, anyway." Then he paid for his stamps, stuffed them in his pocket, and was gone.

July 25

By means of judicious eavesdropping, I have discovered that although Geraldine has left her father's home, she has not vanished altogether off the face of the earth. She has moved to a room in another part of the city. If I wait long enough, and if I listen very attentively, I will discover where she is. Maybe Elliot will hand in a letter directed to her new address — a cheque, perhaps, or a note of apology. Even if it contains accusations and anger, I will have learned her last name and where to find her. And then I will know exactly what to do.

I see Elliot often. He still eats Sara Lee chocolate cake and dilutes his gin with tonic. His brows continue to be drawn together in either anxiety or displeasure, and there is no spring in his step as he shuffles along. Priority Post parcels continue to arrive, as do registered letters. These he receives without the faintest sign of delight or even of curiosity. He seems not yet to have written a letter to his daughter. This is discouraging, but not overwhelmingly so. The present is now full of challenges and possibilities. I greet the start of each day with enormous interest.

S. GARIBALDI
D LEONARDO

MRS. GARIBALDI WAS SMALL, shy, and old. She had thin grey hair that refused to curl, even when she paid forty-five dollars at the Venus Observed Beauty Parlour. It projected in sparse strands from around her wrinkled little face, and she was forever pushing bobby pins into it to keep the wisps in place. As a result, her head was covered with a variety of pins and combs, as well as straight sprouts of hair appearing in strange places, even right on top of her head or behind her left ear.

Mrs. Garibaldi was unhappy. After moving into the Peaceful Villas Home for Senior Citizens, she had quickly discovered that this was not at all where she wanted to be. She just sat in her room and glumphed. That took a lot less energy than going out in the halls to meet people. Besides, Mrs. Garibaldi had always been secretly afraid of strangers, and Peaceful Villas Home was full of them. Three times a day, she went downstairs and ate meals with the other people. She would sit down at the table, look at her plate, frown, and eat her meal in silence. She thought that everyone was very unfriendly. For their part, the guests at her table knew that they had never seen anyone as stuck-up and cross as Mrs. Garibaldi. They didn't know that she had given the best birthday parties ever held in Sinclair County. How could they know that her chocolate chip cookies had made her famous all over Campbellford? And that her head was full, one could almost say bulging, with funny stories? All they could see was the scowl above her spectacles and her eyes focused on her corned beef hash.

Mrs. Garibaldi was living at Peaceful Villas because her son was moving to Vancouver and was worried about her. She would have liked to go to Vancouver, too. After all, she had never seen the mountains. Besides, most of her old Campbellford friends had left town, died, or become too sick or old to move around and pay visits. Vancouver sounded like a nice place. She had heard that the Pacific Ocean was at its doorstep, that there was a famous bridge with an unusual name she couldn't remember, that one could have picnics in a big park with enormous trees and giant totem poles. And she would have been close to her grandchildren. But Victor had said that the relocation would be too hard on her, although she suspected he did not know every single thing there was to know.

Mrs. Garibaldi's eyes filled with tears when she thought about her grandchildren. There were so many of them — six, to be exact. And there were at least four of them who were always ready to be hugged. And the baby. You could hug a baby continually without feeling as though you were taking up his time or getting in the way. But Gillian, Victor's wife, had not felt that hugging the baby all the time was such a wonderful idea. She kept saying that he needed sleep, although Mrs. Garibaldi could not see why, if a baby was lying still and quiet, with a smile spread all over his beautiful face, you need worry about his need for sleep. Mrs. Garibaldi was not stupid. She knew that what was really bothering Gillian was that she was afraid she would drop the baby. It was true that she often dropped things like milk cartons (on the way to the fridge), or her handbag (as she left the bus), or piles of diapers (when she was helping out). But she would have died before she would have let that baby fall. Mrs. Garibaldi looked around her room. It was full of her own furniture; it also contained her dome clock, her statue of Our Lady, her musical jewelry box, and her sterling silver mirror. But not one single thing to hug.

In Mrs. Garibaldi's old apartment building, a little two-year-old boy had lived next door. She could hug him almost any time she wanted, and his mother never seemed to think that he needed sleep. Mrs. Garibaldi would have liked to stay in the apartment. She told Victor this, as soon as he told her she didn't really want to move to Vancouver. But Victor had said, "No, Mother. I know what's best for you. You'd be lonely with us gone. And I wouldn't be here to keep an eye on things."

She knew very well what he meant by keeping an eye on things. She hadn't liked the way, at the end of his nightly phone call, that he always said, "Is the stove off, Mother? Is the iron unplugged? Have you locked your door?" She was willing to admit that she had started a little fire once with the iron, but it had only been a small fire and she had put it out very efficiently with the kettle, which had been full of water at the time. And she couldn't see why you needed to lock the door in a quiet town like Campbellford. He kept saying that there might be some dangerous thugs downtown in the evenings, but she felt that if you thought about misery all the time, you could expect to experience just exactly that. Besides, she didn't live downtown.

And Victor kept mentioning her memory. He had worried

that she might forget this, that, or the other thing. Like Gillian's birthday, or her doctor's appointment, or the name of his supervisor's wife. He even scolded her about her memory. Maybe not scolded, but he did sound so exasperated.

"Mother. Listen." He would begin quietly, and so patiently that she knew something bad was coming. He would be sitting there beside her, doing what she called The Son Thing, with his hand on her shoulder (a poor excuse for a hug), his eyes earnest. "Mother," he would repeat, "try to remember to turn off the bath water. I don't think you really try."

He was no doubt thinking of that insignificant little flood last month, which hadn't done any real permanent damage. And what did that young whippersnapper of forty summers know about trying? She could hardly wait for his own memory to start sliding away from him. But that might not be for another twenty-five years, and she'd be 108 years old by then, or not around to enjoy it. Or to say, "I told you so."

Mrs. Garibaldi's mind felt to her like a black hard-shelled water beetle, scuttling over the surface of things, never dipping down into the still deep waters, never leaving a path in its wake. How could you explain something like that to someone like Victor, who was a computer expert, who kept things in his head that she didn't even dare think about? How could she explain that sometimes her mind floundered around in a grey fog, where the edges of things, of thought, of memories, were not clear? And how could he be expected to understand that trying had nothing whatsoever to do with it? Still, it irritated her.

One would have thought, to hear Victor speak, that no one else had ever been young before. It might do him good to think about being even younger than he was at the present time. If his own memory was so wonderful, he might set it to work remembering the day Harold McInnes had stolen his school bag in Grade One, and he had come home crying and looking for hugs. Or the way he had always been frightened of Hallowe'en night until she made him see how much fun it was. Or the year he had his heart set on playing hockey, but couldn't skate. Mr. Garibaldi had been born in Italy and couldn't even have walked over the ice, but she was from the Lakehead, and knew how. So it was she who had put on her skates and taken him out on the ice to teach him. And now he was talking to her as though she couldn't even fill her own bathtub.

Anyway, Victor had made all the arrangements. Having said that it would be too big an adjustment for her to move to Vancouver, he then turned around and installed her in Toronto. This, he said — and she was sure he meant it — was so she could enjoy the facilities of the nicest possible home he could find. But her foggy mind could detect just the trace of a logical flaw somewhere.

As the weeks went by in Peaceful Villas, Mrs. Garibaldi's attitude towards life did not improve. The more fainthearted and lonely she became, the more she frowned and looked ahead, her eyes centred on nothing. And of course the more she did this, the more unfriendly the other guests thought she was. When Mr. Ambrose came stumbling down the hall on his walker, she did not throw him a friendly hello, or even a smile. When Miss Taylor, the Recreation Director, asked her if she would like to join the expedition to Niagara Falls (or the art gallery or the music festival or the hockey game or the flower show), she tended to recoil, as though physically struck. Genuinely frightened, she always answered, "Oh, no!" Not even "No, thank you." Or "Thank you very much, but I think not today." Just plain "Oh, no!" And when Mrs. Chan came in one day to offer her a chocolate chip cookie, she actually said, "No, thank you. They disagree with me. Besides, I used to make much better ones myself." It is true that she had legitimate indigestion at the time, but courtesy shouldn't be dependent on one's stomach.

To give credit where due, this speech to Mrs. Chan was one of the things Mrs. Garibaldi had no difficulty in remembering. Its tone of rudeness and ingratitude rang in her ears for weeks, particularly at three o'clock in the morning. But her guilt compounded her shyness, and it became almost impossible for her to venture forth beyond her own threshold, except for meals. And what with all this brooding and going about her business (or lack of it) with eyes downcast, the other inmates of Peaceful Villas felt not the slightest desire to approach her. Even the overzealous Miss Taylor — so oppressively young, so immaculately dressed in white tailored blouses and grey flannel pants — wearied of asking her to join the group. If the old thing wanted to be snobby, let her. Let her take her pincushion head and keep it in her own room if that was what she chose to do. Miss Taylor wasn't going to be friendly anymore to someone who obviously had never, her whole life long, learned how to smile.

Mrs. Chan did make one last effort to penetrate Mrs. Garibaldi's inhospitable shell. This was difficult for her, but she felt compelled to make at least one more move in Mrs. Garibaldi's direction. She herself had suffered acutely during her first weeks at Peaceful Villas, from just plain loneliness, and from being a second-generation Chinese-Canadian. That meant slim hips (which had alienated her from the plump ladies who were encased in corsets and complexes), and high collars, and eyes and skin unlike any of the other guests. She knew what it was to feel on the outskirts of all the action. She would forget, or at least forgive, the episode of the chocolate chip cookies, and try one more time.

When Mrs. Chan arrived at her door, Mrs. Garibaldi opened it with uncommon swiftness, having been standing beside it sorting her handkerchiefs at the time. Mrs. Garibaldi had heard about the way entire lifetimes pass before people's eyes, just before drowning. She would not have anticipated a similar experience upon being confronted by Mrs. Chan. While a good thirty seconds ticked away, she saw in her mind's eye, in rapid succession, scene after scene involving chocolate chip cookies and her success in the baking and serving of them. Then she witnessed again her own terrible gaff and the fruitless weeks of regret following her display of bad manners. And there, in front of her, obviously holding out an olive branch, was Mrs. Chan. Here was an opportunity to make amends, to humble herself in a suitable and attractive way.

Mrs. Garibaldi's momentary delight at this prospect was followed by the terrible realization that she had left her teeth, all twenty-eight of them, in her bathroom. She had coped more or less successfully all her life with her unruly hair. Unaware of the advent of punk rock and the invention of hair gel, she believed that her head was different from all others, and she had long ago come to terms with this fact. But to appear in public *toothless*! To make an apology is difficult enough at the best of times; to do this while looking like a Hallowe'en witch was more than Mrs. Garibaldi could face. Mumbling something entirely incoherent, but which, if translated, would have been, "I'm truly sorry, Mrs. Chan, but would you mind very much returning in ten minutes?", she closed the door on Mrs. Chan's brave and expectant face.

Mrs. Chan stood there for a lengthy moment, staring at the closed door. Then she turned abruptly, and all her oriental reserve deserted her. With every ounce of force that she could pour into her small right foot, she kicked the hall wastebasket so hard that it hit the wall at the far end of the corridor. Fury was filling her so absolutely that there was not a millimeter left for anything else. She strode down to the common room on her tiny legs, eager to tell her tale to the waiting ladies.

Back in her room, Mrs. Garibaldi affixed her teeth, put on her best powder-blue wool dress (chosen with remarkable success by Gillian), and even tried smoothing down her hair.

Then she sat down and waited, rehearsing a gracious little speech of apology for past and present sins. But Mrs. Chan, of course, failed to appear. Mrs. Garibaldi pretended not to have heard the lunch bell when it rang. Absences from meals were frowned on, but after all, she was quite deaf and could be expected to miss a bell or two. She was still sitting in the chair when she dropped off to sleep at three in the afternoon. At five, the bell sounded once more. Sighing, Mrs. Garibaldi rose stiffly from her chair and went down to the dining room. She did not look to the right or to the left. She ate her meal in silence, as usual. She prided herself on her self-control. Among Canadians of Italian origin, her ability to curb her emotions had been regarded as something of a marvel. But to her horror, one large wet tear suddenly slid down her face and dropped, plop, into her mushroom soup. From the end of the table, Mrs. Chan observed that tear, but it was not enough to make her move an inch in Mrs. Garibaldi's direction. It was perhaps just enough to make her feel a little bit pleased. Let her suffer. Nasty little woman.

Mrs. Garibaldi's life did not improve as the weeks went by. Victor, through some genetic or psychological mutation, had escaped the Italian traits of warmth and effusiveness; he almost never wrote to her. Occasionally (on Valentine's Day, at Eastertime, on her birthday), he would phone, but the calls were depressingly full of instructions and advice. Had she had a medical checkup? Was she eating her green leafy vegetables? (There would then follow a sermon on calcium and osteoporosis and a caution about falling.) Was she taking her daily walk around the block? (Indeed she was not, but she was certainly not going to tell him so. Despite a lifelong horror of lying, she now resorted to it.) "Yes," she said firmly. "In fact, twice a day. I feel absolutely blooming."

It was hard to connect Victor's matter-of-fact efficient voice with the chubby preschooler he had once been, with the warm brown eyes and the damp black curls — damp from forever running around investigating life with an energy and an urgency that was passionate and open. To have given birth to this one perfect child at age forty-three was still, forty years later, a miracle to her. Her arms ached for the pleasure of holding him, of feeling his soft child-flesh melt into her chest and her lap. She thought sardonically of notices stuck to the back bumpers of cars: "Have you hugged your child today?" She invented a new sign, and mentally affixed it to every car, every lamppost, every billboard in Toronto: "Have you hugged your mother today?" Asterisk. Regardless of age.

Gillian did write. Every week. Mrs. Garibaldi appreciated this in a thin kind of way. Obviously Gillian set aside a certain time on a specific day to write The Letter. It was short and matter-of-fact, and there were no XX's and OO's at the end. Victor is well. Johnny has started nursery school. (But does he like it? Is he happy? What does he say? Who are his friends? Does he send a hug?) My work with the United Appeal keeps me busy. Victor's job requires that we travel a good deal. (But not to Toronto, I notice.) Mrs. Garibaldi was grateful for The Letter, and said so. But when the postman arrived with it, she did not rush into her room, breathless, to rip it open.

✳

One day in midsummer, when the room was particularly hot, as only a steamy Toronto day can be, Mrs. Garibaldi looked at her open window and wondered how she could encourage the entrance of that breeze that was ruffling the leaves in the back garden of Peaceful Villas. With remarkable ease, given the arthritic condition of her hands, she clicked a couple of small levers and removed the screen from the window, laying it carefully on the floor beside her sewing basket. The breeze did indeed flow more smoothly into the room, and she congratulated herself on her ingenuity and dexterity. She sat down and worked on her crossword puzzle in front of the window, feeling comfortable for the first time since the start of the heat wave. The coolness more than compensated for the few wasps that wandered in; houseflies were no problem if there was no food to tempt them, and mosquitoes never bit her anyway — "not delicious enough," she mused ruefully.

She eased herself out of the chair painfully when she heard the lunch bell. She had discovered that deafness was no excuse for failure to appear at lunch. One was expected to have a clock, and one was urged to refer to it often. She laid her crossword puzzle on the beige comforter on her bed. Comforter. Duvets, they called them nowadays. Victor and Gillian had given it to her last Christmas. It was warm, and basically a well-chosen gift. Old bones, she had discovered, needed heat. But why beige? It was of course Gillian's favourite colour, but Mrs. Garibaldi loved blue. And orange. Secretly, she loved hot pink. She was lucid enough to recognize that the Victors and Gillians of this world frown upon hot pink. It shared the stigma of lime green, certain shades of royal blue, and fire-engine red. Vulgar. But oh so beautiful, so warming and cheering to the eye and spirit.

When Mrs. Garibaldi returned from lunch, she entered the room, burping quietly to herself. Time for her afternoon nap, an event that marked the cessation of effort and even of thought, an easing of sore tired muscles — and if she was lucky, it also meant the loss of consciousness, the sinking ease of sleep. She thought about death, not without pleasure.

Mrs. Garibaldi stopped short as she approached the bed. There, comfortably sunk into the duvet, his head pressed onto her crossword puzzle, was what Mrs. Garibaldi was later to describe as "the biggest cat in the world." No kitten this. No cunning, cuddlesome creature, eager to frolic and play. This was a CAT. Large, firm, thick of fur, and richly whiskered, he had not been a kitten for a very long time. He was a deep lush grey, from tip of ear to end of tail.

Mrs. Garibaldi sat down on the bed very carefully. She had forgotten about cats. She had forgotten about how she felt about cats. Victor had been allergic to everything with fur or feathers, and cats had gone out of her life with his arrival — a small price to pay for that soft and loving child. For the first time in many weeks, Mrs. Garibaldi smiled. Then, tentatively, softly, she placed her hand on the cat's back. She knew that some cats are skittish and hate to be touched. She also knew that other cats are calm and consoling, craving physical contact, giving back the comfort that they seek. Mrs. Garibaldi whispered aloud, "Oh please, please, *please!*"

The sleeping cat murmured a deep soothing sound and tensed his limbs, not savagely (which could, she knew, have been the case), but lazily, blissfully. Then his purr, that symphony of the throat and chest, so comforting to lovers of cats, began its low and lovely song. Her prayers answered, Mrs. Garibaldi watched as he rose to his full height, stretched once more, and then sank deeply and satisfyingly into her lap. He was warm and nourishing; he was also instantly asleep. Mrs. Garibaldi's arthritic body was in an uncomfortable position. Nonetheless, she continued to sit there with the cat in her lap, her hungry hands stroking his back, her congealed heart stirring, her spirit knowing a forgotten peace. She stayed in this position until the cat woke up, thirty minutes later. Then she picked up his heavy body and held him close. Some cats hold themselves away from you when this is done. Others lay their heads on your chest and press themselves into your body. It was this latter kind of cat that Mrs. Garibaldi was now holding. Chuckling, she muttered, "Have you hugged your cat today?"

Depression longs for nothing unless perhaps for the end of depression. So it had been for Mrs. Garibaldi during the first nine weeks at Peaceful Villas. She had never in all that time coveted a pretty dress, or longed for a new gold chain, or hungered for a good novel, or even hankered after a mint pattie. Suddenly Mrs. Garibaldi found herself longing for something. She longed to possess that cat. While she had sat there, waiting for him to wake up, she had already named him. Leonardo. Rising with a stiffness that she did not even notice, she closed the window. Just for an hour or so she would enjoy him. She would ignore that tag — obviously some sort of identification — on his collar. This cat, this Leonardo, obviously was owned by someone. But they could wait. This afternoon, just for this one short afternoon, she needed him more than his owners did. At suppertime she would let him go.

So Mrs. Garibaldi spent the afternoon with Leonardo. But first she slipped out the door, locked it carefully, and walked two blocks to Sam's Variety Store for a half-litre of milk. She also bought a small bowl (a pretty one, with blue flowers on the rim) and a package of dry cat food, *just in case*. Then, after two gratifying and very hot hours with Leonardo, she gave him a farewell hug, opened the window, and let him go.

Despite her recent bereavement, Mrs. Garibaldi was inclined to feel cheerful at suppertime. She smiled at Mrs. McCurdy, newly arrived just yesterday, and the woman looked startled but pleased. Mrs. McCurdy had been warned about Mrs. Garibaldi almost the moment she had crossed the threshold of Peaceful Villas, and here the lady was actually looking tender. Mrs. Garibaldi ate her chili and cole slaw with considerable appetite and returned to her room with unusual haste.

He was back. Once more stationed on the duvet, he was settled down, green eyes wide open, in the sphinx position. Mrs. Garibaldi smiled softly, and prepared his dinner. Then she did what she knew she had to do. Never, her whole life long, had she been one to avoid reality. When her husband had developed inoperable cancer of the liver, she had not pretended for one moment that he was going to get better; when the doctor had told her that she would have no more children, she had ceased to count the weeks between periods; when Victor came home and announced his engagement to Gillian, she had given up hoping that he would marry a warm and dark-eyed Italian-Canadian girl. What had to be had to be. Her one failure in accepting life had been in her reaction to Peaceful Villas — but then Peaceful Villas had been more or less foisted on her.

Mrs. Garibaldi sighed as she approached Leonardo, pencil and paper in hand. With her magnifying glass, she inspected the tag on his collar. After recording the name and phone number, she rose painfully from the edge of the bed and walked across the room to the phone. She dialed the number and waited.

"Yes?"

"May I speak to Mr. or Mrs. Jefferson?" Mrs. Garibaldi said.

"I'm sorry," said the clear, clipped voice. "They've moved. We have their old number until the phone company comes to disconnect it."

Mrs. Garibaldi allowed herself to hope. "Where have they moved to?"

"I have no idea," said the voice, with all the personal interest of a recorded announcement. "I only know that they've left the country. Diplomatic service. Somewhere in South America, I think they said. The post office is looking after forwarding their mail. You could try them."

Mrs. Garibaldi had no intention of trying them. Let the Jeffersons enjoy the monkeys and snakes or whatever else they might find in Brazil or Chile or Ecuador. They certainly didn't need a cat, and quarantine laws were strict. She was smiling so hard that she forgot to say goodbye.

Mrs. Garibaldi was now faced with a problem that was more complicated than any she had encountered for many years. Victor was not here to tell her what to do, and for the first time in many months, she was forced to do her own thinking. Her problem was not small. How do you keep a cat in a building that categorically forbids the keeping of pets?

Mrs. Garibaldi had never ventured forth on the subway since moving to Toronto. The mere thought of it terrified her. But there are terrors and terrors. Her fear of losing Leonardo made the subway look very simple, even benevolent. It was the means of getting downtown to buy a litter box. This involved asking directions. Well, she could do that. Approaching the cool Miss Taylor, she asked how one bought tickets, where the stop was, how to get off. More than a little taken aback, Miss Taylor nonetheless recognized this as a forward step by Mrs. Garibaldi, and chose not to ask any questions. She gave her the necessary directions and returned to her own business.

It was an exciting if alarming journey for Mrs. Garibaldi. She liked the row upon row of people lined up on the subway seats, white, black, yellow, fat, thin, serene, anxious. She wondered about them, and felt she could tell which were widows, which were lucky enough to have chubby children to cuddle and put to bed, which ones had the nervous jitters. She loved the speed and clatter of the train, and was reading the advertisements so avidly that she almost missed her stop.

Getting off at Yonge and Dundas, she climbed up the long flight of stairs to the street, and found herself on The Strip. White and weary, she leaned against a *Star* dispenser box, and closed her eyes.

"Are you okay, lady?" asked a voice, and Mrs. Garibaldi opened her eyes to see a young face with startling eyelashes and scarlet lipstick peering anxiously at her. But it was her hair that captivated her. Sticking straight up in sculpted wisps and peaks (like the meringue on a lemon pie, she thought), it was black, with a streak of the wildest red down the centre.

"Fine, my dear, just fine," she panted, patting her own spiky hair. "But those stairs were certainly not made with *me* in mind."

The girl took her by the hand and led her across the street. "Lookit, Granny," she said, giving her a little squeeze. "If you go out through the Eaton Centre exit, you can come all the way up by escalator. And you wouldn't have to go anywhere else. This is it. You can find everything you need, right in here. Everything."

"Like a litter box?"

"A what?"

"A cat's bathroom," Mrs. Garibaldi said, wondering how she

would find such a specialized item in this jungle of stores and people.

"C'mon, love," said her new friend. She steered her in the direction of the pet store. "Gotta split right now, but that guy'll help you." Depositing her at the door, she rushed off, leather coat shining, metal studs gleaming.

"Hey, girl!" Mrs. Garibaldi called after her. "I like your hair."

The girl turned around and grinned. "Thanks, Granny. I think yours is pretty neat, too."

Pretty neat! Mrs. Garibaldi had heard that expression often enough to know it was a compliment. She walked a little straighter as she entered the pet store.

Two hours later, Mrs. Garibaldi was back in her room, shredding newspaper into the litter box — just in time, evidently, because Leonardo walked right in, adjusted himself with quiet dignity, and did what he apparently had to do. Litter could come later.

Mrs. Garibaldi had had enough adventures for one day. She collapsed on the bed without even taking off her hat. As she was dropping off, she realized that she had gone all the way downtown in her bedroom slippers. Leonardo's grey body was pressed into her side. The music of his purr lulled her to sleep.

"I cannot do this alone." Mrs. Garibaldi was speaking out loud to herself, or possibly to Leonardo. It was one week after the subway trip, and she could see that her venture was more complicated than she'd thought it would be. Leonardo was a big cat, needing exercise and fresh air. He also had a strident and penetrating voice. Litter disposal was becoming a problem. So was *lack* of disposal. Mrs. Garibaldi could not be forever spraying Lysol into the air. The threat of discovery hung over her, by day and by night. More frightening than the subway was the thought that she was going to have to infiltrate the clientele of Peaceful Villas in search of an ally. But if it had to be done, it had to be done.

That day, she went down to lunch with her loins girded. Sitting down at the table, she looked around at the seven other faces and smiled brightly at each one. Almost nobody smiled back. "Lovely day!" she ventured. Something like a murmur of assent could be heard, a sort of universal positive grunt. But no one said, for instance, "Why, yes, Mrs. Garibaldi, it certainly is!" Down at the far end of the table, Mrs. Chan made a conscious effort to offer nothing, not even a grunt. She ate her baked beans with care, her eyes fixed on her plate.

Mrs. Garibaldi could see that this was not going to be easy. However, she tried to do all the right things — things that she had ignored until that moment. She passed the salt. She praised the beans. She asked Mr. Ambrose if he would care for a little more salad. She said, "Oh, isn't that just lovely!" when Mrs. Giles announced that her daughter was coming to visit her that afternoon. She started to sense a softening in the air, very slight, but unmistakable. Finally, she asked, ever so casually, "Do any of you like cats?"

Mrs. Chan raised her eyes involuntarily from her plate. She loved cats. She *adored* cats. She was the original Egyptian, by way of Peking. But there was no way, cats notwithstanding, that she was going to bend.

The replies varied. "Oh, *yes!*" Miss Thompson crooned,

hands clasped over her enormous bosom. "I had a ginger cat for thirteen years before he passed on. Such a comfort. Such a sorrow." Then she added, by way of explanation, "My apartment was on the sixteenth floor."

"Cats are generic," said Mrs. Timmins, who fancied herself a mine of information on all subjects. She pushed her glasses up on her nose and straightened up in her chair. "They're all basically alike. Same rubbing, arching, kneading, stretching. A most intriguing animal, and possibly a lot more intelligent than we suppose. But *like?* I don't believe one *likes* animals. Certainly one does not *love* them."

Mrs. Chan had a hard time letting *that* remark slide by. She shot Mrs. Timmins a look of undisguised distaste, but that was all she would allow herself. Several others gave their opinions of cats, some glowing, some scathing. Mrs. Giles slapped the table top and exclaimed, "Oh, how I wish they would keep a cat, just *one*, in this building!"

Mrs. Chan looked at Mrs. Giles with an expression of such intense longing that Mrs. Garibaldi felt it was time to gamble. She waited until Mrs. Chan went back to her room. It was number 324. She had checked. She took the elevator up to the third floor, found the room, and knocked at the door. While she waited for Mrs. Chan to answer, she took a long deep breath, counted to fifteen, and then let it out slowly.

When Mrs. Chan opened the door, there was no long pause. Mrs. Garibaldi held firmly to the side of the door, and spoke.

"Mrs. Chan," she said, trying without success to keep her voice smooth and confident. "I feel quite certain that your chocolate chip cookies are a hundred times more delicious than any I have ever made. I had a stomachache that day, which of course is no excuse. And possibly you did not realize about my teeth. They were in the bathroom. Victor would have been horrified. I put on my best powder-blue dress and waited. Four hours. Mrs. Chan. I have a cat in my room."

Mrs. Chan hesitated for only an instant. She bowed slightly and said, "Please come in."

Mrs. Garibaldi's courage bore remarkable fruit. Mrs. Chan received her courteously, and produced a tentative smile. She displayed a reined-in interest in Mrs. Garibaldi's problem. But her visit to Leonardo later in the afternoon removed every last defence that she had so carefully cultivated. Face aglow, her arms full of cat, she pledged unlimited time and effort to his protection.

When Mrs. Chan rose to leave, Mrs. Garibaldi said, "Mrs. Chan. I do know that orientals have a rather cool way of looking at things. Or of expressing them. However, I will have to tell you that to an Italian-Canadian, a moment like this calls for an embrace. I wonder if I might hug you."

Mrs. Chan bowed once again. "Please do," she said.

Mrs. Chan and Mrs. Garibaldi proved to be an impressive team — intelligent, inventive, forceful. They organized the cat lovers of Peaceful Villas, and devised complicated schedules for visiting Leonardo, for litter disposal, for the purchase and delivery of food. Mrs. Garibaldi was no longer lonely. In fact, on Remembrance Day, when Victor called, the room was so full of people that she had to ask him to call another day, when she might be less busy.

She and her guests were to reach a number of important decisions about Leonardo during that meeting. The group had come to order at about ten a.m. Mrs. Chan was in the chair. She had been elected President by acclamation, and had demonstrated a fine combination of administrative and pragmatic skills. She was able to remain calm in the face of conflicting points of view and could keep the agenda from spilling out at the sides. Mrs. Garibaldi had been chosen Supervisor of Activities, a nice vague title that meant she was in on just about everything.

Mr. Ambrose was Treasurer, and successfully administered the funds for any of Leonardo's extra needs — catnip mice, rabies shots, the two stitches in his ear the time he got into a half-opened tin of salmon, an electric can opener to make sure that this would never happen again. Mrs. Garibaldi paid for all the food and litter, it being more or less accepted that Leonardo was her cat. Mrs. Timmins, who at first refused to join "any emotional cat lovers association," finally allied herself to the group "for the pure intellectual interest." She became the Transportation Director. She was a confident if not always competent driver, and had a small car. It was she who bundled Leonardo into a large picnic hamper and took him back and forth to the vet, humming loud patriotic songs ("Land of Hope and Glory," "La Marseillaise") as she went by the receptionist, in case any unusual sounds should issue from the basket. Mrs. Giles told Mrs. Garibaldi, in strictest confidence, that she had heard Mrs. Timmins talking baby talk to the picnic hamper one day when she was putting it in the car.

But then, everything that went on in the Cat Club was in the strictest confidence. This became just one of the many anxieties of the enterprise. Being cat lovers, the members of the group were genuinely troubled by Leonardo's need for fresh air, by the fact that he was unable to exercise his beautiful body. And of course they were all fearful of what would happen if they should be caught harbouring an animal on the premises. They had all read the constitution of Peaceful Villas and were only

too familiar with the rules and with the penalties for infringe-
ment. To be honest, most of them were also genuinely appre-
hensive about the reactions of the assorted sons and daughters
and nieces and nephews in the event of a general public expo-
sure. This November 11th meeting had been called in the hope
of solving some of these problems.

Oddly enough, it was Miss Thompson who came up with the
remedy for their ills. Mrs. Garibaldi was to shiver when she
recalled that she had considered not asking Miss Thompson to
join. She looked so sleepy and blubbery that somehow she felt
that she must be stupid. And possibly too effusive for safety.
(Victor's attitude towards her own abilities skittered across
Mrs. Garibaldi's mind as she mused about this.) Highly emotional herself, she had a feeling of great uneasiness when in the
presence of excessive emotion. How could one be sure, she had
argued, that Miss Thompson would not, literally, let the cat
out of the bag?

But no. It was Miss Thompson who saved the day. It was her
suggestion that they start a mouse rumour.

The method was absurdly simple. They simply talked about
mice. This they did when in the presence of members of the
Administration (the Executive Director, the cool Miss Taylor,
the Dietitian, the Health Adviser), and they did it with remarkable subtlety. They didn't talk *to* the administrators. They just
made sure that they were heard. The snatches of conversation,
when combined with other bits and pieces of talk, added up to
an unmistakable crisis.

"Oh! *Really?* And she's so *frightened* of mice!"

"Heavens! *Two* in the same *room?* I'd a thousand times sooner
meet two lions!"

"My doctor says that mice are unhealthy. He says that mice
mean *dirt*."

"I can't imagine where they're coming from. It's a regular epidemic."

"I just hope that Victor doesn't find out. He'd have me out of here in two minutes."

Finally, the Administration stopped discussing the problem in private and held a general house meeting. Mr. Endicott, the Executive Director, addressed the group, his eyes rimmed with pink, his nose shining. "Unhappily," he began, leaning heavily on the word, "we seem to have a few little mice in the building."

What he was thinking was that they had a small *army* of mice, but that kind of comment could give rise to extravagant repercussions among the families of the guests, and in the offices of the City Health Department. He fiddled nervously with his Medic Alert bracelet.

"Yes," he said, "a few little mice. And we feel we have to tell you this because we're going to set up a series of traps and plates of mouse seed throughout the building. These will be centred mainly in the residential area, because it seems that this is where they are concentrated."

Mr. Endicott offered a toothy smile to the sea of white heads before him. "So keep all your bare toes out of those traps, and don't let anyone get the idea that the mouse seeds are sunflower seeds. They're for *mice*, not *people*, and they'll be on the *floor*." He chuckled uneasily, hopeful of his wit.

"I wish he wouldn't talk to us as though we were in the remedial section of Grade One," grumbled Mr. Ambrose.

A week passed. The rumours continued, in fact increased, and one had the feeling that mice were outnumbering people by about five to one. But the traps bore no fruit, and the bowls of mouse seed remained untasted. The Administration was visibly shaken. One unfortunate comment, one single injudicious word uttered outside Peaceful Villas, and the place could be condemned or closed within days. The Executive Director was looking pale and was said to have lost his appetite. The Cat Club felt that the time was ripe. Mrs. Garibaldi was delegated to go and speak to Mr. Endicott in private on Saturday afternoon.

Mrs. Garibaldi was splendid. In fact, she found herself wishing that Victor could see her in this her finest hour. Victor did love her. She could see that now. But he didn't really *admire* her very much anymore. And on this particular afternoon, it was Mrs. Garibaldi's opinion that she was undeniably admirable.

"I understand," she said oh so carefully to Mr. Endicott, "that you haven't caught any mice."

Mr. Endicott lowered his eyes, but said nothing. He did, however, sigh.

"Well," Mrs. Garibaldi continued, "I would not for the world intrude, but I have had a little experience or two with mice in my time, and I thought you might be interested in hearing about what I have come to look upon as a foolproof method of getting rid of them" She waited.

Mr. Endicott raised his eyes. Something like hope appeared in them. "Mrs. Garibaldi," he began, clenching and unclenching his fingers. "Be good enough to make yourself clear. If you can rid us of those . . . few mice . . . please do."

"Well," Mrs. Garibaldi ventured, "it's not *me* who can do it for you. I can just offer a solution. Perhaps the *only* solution."

"Which is what, Mrs. Garibaldi?" Mr. Endicott stood up now to his full five feet four and one-half inches. "Is *what?*"

Mrs. Garibaldi looked Mr. Endicott full in the eyes and answered.

"A cat."

It is amazing how quickly a rule can be broken — or read-justed, as Mr. Endicott preferred to phrase it — when people are in a state of fear. And Mr. Endicott, if truth be told, was scared right out of his wits by mice. He would not for all the world have admitted this, even to his closest friend, and certainly not to his overconfident wife, but the fact was that for several weeks, ever since the rumours had started, he had scarcely shut his eyes at night. The fears some people have about heights or enclosed spaces or snakes, Mr. Endicott had about mice. He would do almost anything to deliver himself and the building from this curse.

"It's Saturday afternoon, Mrs. Garibaldi. Not a good time to procure a cat. On Monday, perhaps." Secretly he was thinking, *If I can just survive that long.*

"Why, so it is indeed Saturday afternoon! What a pity." Mrs. Garibaldi paused for a moment. "Do you know? I might be able to help you. And before Monday. That is, if the idea appeals to you."

Mr. Endicott checked a desire to jump up and down. "It appeals to me," he said.

"I know of a cat who lives quite near here. He is huge and strong, and would, I am confident, make an excellent mouser."

"But the owners?" Mr. Endicott discovered that he was holding his breath.

"Have left the country. The kind lady who is looking after him is doing so under difficult circumstances. She would be quite willing to give him up if she could find a safe and compassionate home for him."

"You do know, Mrs. Garibaldi," said Mr. Endicott, conscious that he must cover all bases, "that this animal would have to be kept in the residence wing. Do you think the guests could cope with that?"

"I think we could cope with that."

"You're certain?"

"Well," said Mrs. Garibaldi, "think of it this way. If you had your choice between one cat and a battalion of mice, which would you choose?"

Mr. Endicott coughed. "Mrs. Garibaldi, I would be enormously grateful if you could bring me the animal this very afternoon. If it would not be too great an imposition."

"I believe," Mrs. Garibaldi said, hesitating ever so slightly, "that this could be arranged without a great deal of inconvenience."

"And Mrs. Garibaldi . . ."

"Yes?"

"I hate to ask even one more favour of you, but do you suppose you can think of anyone among the guests who would be willing to take on the responsibility for the care and feeding of the cat? Perhaps in our large group we might be able to find one cat lover."

Mrs. Garibaldi was unable to repress a large and radiant smile. "I'm sure we can find someone," she said, resisting the desire to pat Mr. Endicott's nervous hands. "If no one volunteers, I would be quite willing to take this on myself."

Already Mr. Endicott was looking less pale. Walking over to where Mrs. Garibaldi was standing, he shook her hand, and then put one arm around her shoulders in what Mrs. Garibaldi felt could be defined as a hug.

"Thank you, Mrs. Garibaldi," he said.

❋

Two nights later, Victor phoned. "Mother," he said, "a home for Seniors has just opened in West Vancouver. I thought I'd put in an application for you. What do you think?"

Mrs. Garibaldi did have a fleeting sense of regret when she thought about all those grandchildren. And of course about Victor. Then she said, "Thank you, Victor. That's very kind of you. But no."

There was a moment of silence. Then he spoke. "Mother, we can keep an eye on you here. Gillian will have you to dinner occasionally. We can go for drives. The climate is milder. I'm sure you'll be glad you made the move. Just leave the details to me."

"Thank you, Victor dear, but I'm keeping my own eye on me rather nicely here. And I'm needed."

"You're what, Mother? What was that you said?"

"Never mind, dear," said Mrs. Garibaldi. Victor was sweet, but he couldn't be expected to understand. "And Victor, do you know that Mr. Endicott hugged me last Saturday?"

"Mother, are you sure you're all right? You don't sound quite yourself. Has the doctor seen you recently? Are you happy? And do you have any friends?"

"Yes, Victor, I have dozens of friends, some human, some not."

"Mother! Are you *sure* you're . . ."

"Yes, dear, I'm absolutely sure I'm all right. And now, if you don't mind, I think I'll just hang up and go to dinner. The bell rang a moment ago, and I'm starved. Goodbye Victor, dear. Give my love to the children, and say hello to Gillian. When I find a free moment, I'll answer her letter. I'm very busy."

And then she hung up. Leonardo had been on her lap throughout the conversation. She stroked him absently. Then, sitting very still, she thought about how much she loved Victor. A good son. Who really cared.

But her mind was already on other things. Rising from the chair, she filled Leonardo's bowl with Seanip Dinner before she left the room. "I think I'll buy a hot pink cover for my comforter," she said as she closed the door. "I saw one in the duvet shop the last time I was on Bloor Street." She nodded comfortably, and smiled at Mr. Ambrose as he crept up the hall. "I really feel that I'm too old to start all over again," she said to him. "Besides, there are no subways in Vancouver." Mr. Ambrose nodded. He seemed to think this a reasonable remark. Mrs. Garibaldi gave him a little pat, as they moved along together to the dining room.

"Oh good!" she said. "I think I smell corned beef hash."

MRS. MACINTOSH

EVEN WHEN THOMAS is standing up, his stomach strains against his vest, so you can imagine what it is like when he is sitting down. Normally I have nothing whatsoever against obesity. In fact, there is a comfortable and soft quality about large bodies which I often find appealing. But it is never easy to tolerate pomposity, and I have always felt that a pompous person who is fat is the least attractive kind. If a man is constantly nagging you about your lack of self-discipline, it is irritating to realize that he has no discipline at all in the matter of food. And Thomas has an irritating habit of scratching that stomach in a slow and thoughtful way just before delivering one of his ponderous pronouncements.

As when he said to me one evening at dinner, over the chicken casserole, "Alfreda, I have decided, after careful consideration, that it is time I purchased a suit, possibly two. The calibre of my professionalism requires that my clothing complement my position at the bank. I feel that the quality of a suit reflects the level of one's expertise." All this preceded by that vague, unfunctional scratching.

In the old days when I was younger, when my eyes were shut tight and all critical faculties dormant, I would think, Yes, indeed, an important job needs an important suit. At what point in a marriage, I wonder, does one start to watch and see, and to feel a drawing away? I suppose it varies. In some cases, no doubt, it never happens at all. But how can you live with someone seven days a week for eleven years without eventually spotting, for instance, that he has no idea who he really is? "Take off your mask!" I have sometimes longed to scream. "Take a good look, and then do some heavy stocktaking."

But Thomas's stocktaking was of a different kind, and my screams have always been imaginary.

His mother, I am told, would never permit anyone to call him Tommy or Tom. Mrs. MacIntosh was quick to point out that her father's name had been Thomas MacGregor, and she made it very clear that her respect for his memory was profound. You did not dillydally with Mrs. MacIntosh, even in the matter of names. The first time Thomas took me home to meet her, he introduced me with pride. I was seventeen to his twenty-six, and I was pretty; neither of these facts did anything to increase my popularity with her.

"Mother," he said, puffing himself up even then like a pigeon — although this only occurred to me much later — "I take pleasure in introducing Freddie. Freddie, I'd like you to meet my mother."

She rose from her needlepoint chair, erect and uncompromising, looking at me carefully from tip of scruffed shoes to kinky perm. She smiled a narrow company smile and said, "I'm delighted to meet you. Freddie? Did you say Freddie?"

"Alfreda is her real name," Thomas said. "Her friends call her Freddie."

"Alfreda is a lovely name," she said, coolly. "I will call you Alfreda."

Oh well, I thought, it probably doesn't matter in the slightest, because I can see that you are not likely to be numbered among my friends.

Which turned out to be true. I never did get rid of the sense that my social slip was showing, that I was exactly what she never, in her most reckless moment, would have chosen for a daughter-in-law. To her, I was a piece of insubstantial fluff, blown in from the Yukon, where my father worked as a labourer on a weather station. And I *was* insubstantial. I was torn in too many directions. I raged against my father's drinking bouts, and wished he would clean his fingernails and rein in his temper. I also faulted my mother for not making some of these things happen. But I respected my father's hard work and his fierce pride, and I loved my mother. I swayed with whatever wind blew hardest.

"And just who does that woman think she is, anyway?" I would whisper aloud, when I was back in my rooming house, soaking in the tub. A MacGregor by birth and a MacIntosh by marriage, but from an inferior part of town — no better than my own — and a widow at that. No man to back up all those pretensions with a wallet or a profession. A front porch that needs painting. I would immerse myself in the hot water, and blow a volley of bubbles.

I suppose I was so taken up with Mrs. MacIntosh's glacial pride that I failed to notice that her son shared some of her less attractive characteristics. It was not easy to connect these two people, at first. They looked as though they had not one single gene in common. She was tall and pencil thin. He was of middling height and stocky, muscular and sturdy. The stomach came much later, after he placed three thousand miles between his mother and himself. She would never for one second have permitted that paunch to develop.

But it was his face that was a lie to his parentage. It was round and pleasant; as a small child, he must have been unusually attractive — a dead ringer for any Campbell Soup Kid. There was no way for me to know that with the passage of years he would look more and more like a Pekinese dog. Nor, under different circumstances, would I have minded that fact. But, when you marry a man with a pleasant round face who is kind and attentive, it is a shock to discover, after a while, that you are being treated very sternly by someone who resembles a Pekinese dog.

Pride sits badly on any face, but some people have the looks that can carry arrogance and conceit with a kind of flair. Like Mrs. MacIntosh. Much as I feared and disliked my future mother-in-law, it was not difficult to recognize that she had class. She didn't need wealth in order to make her point in our community. And the point that she obviously wanted to make was that she had come from superior stock. Her posture was not merely flawless. It proclaimed to all who saw her that she was proud of who and what she was. You had to check a tendency to curtsy when she entered a room. What's more, she had the looks to go with this. When I first saw her, I suppose she was about forty-two, and a very young forty-two at that. Her eyes were grey and clear, her nose slender in the bridge, delicately aquiline, straight out of a Van Dyck painting. Her cheek bones were well defined, her chin firm. Her neck was long and still lovely. Crowning all this was a head of prematurely white hair, thick, wavy, elegantly arranged. It mattered not at all that she had only two formal outfits. Had she worn either of them to a Buckingham Palace garden party, heads would have turned. As I looked at her, even at the time of that unfortunate meeting, I kept repeating to myself, *good blood, good blood*. And even while I feared and abhorred what Mrs. MacIntosh represented, I longed to possess that same sure and heady confidence: I wanted to have a share in her legacy.

Of course Mrs. MacIntosh resisted the match with every weapon at her disposal. And her weapons were deadly. Her insults were delivered with a smile — subtle affronts disguised as compliments. If you would like to know how this is done, stand in front of a mirror and smile graciously. Then, maintaining the smile, strive to look superior, pained, and disapproving, all at the same time. She had mastered this technique to perfection. And if I turned up for dinner in my very best dress, purchased especially for the occasion, she could be guaranteed to say something like, "Your shoes are unusually shiny tonight, Alfreda" (smile, smile). This could be interpreted in various ways:

— Shiny shoes are invariably made of plastic or of leather of an inferior quality, or

— Your shoes are usually not shined properly, or

— I am commenting on your shoes in order to avoid mentioning your unfortunate dress.

Or she would say, casually, to Thomas, "Whatever happened to that strikingly beautiful Rose Harrigan? The one who won the scholarship to Oxford? Alfreda, now, has much better skin than Rose." Which could be decoded as "Alfreda is not strikingly beautiful, nor has she won any scholarships lately."

Nonetheless, before I reached my nineteenth birthday, Thomas and I did marry. He was in the grip of a wild infatuation.

I suppose I attracted him because I was so unlike that domineering force who was his mother. I was soft-spoken and self-effacing, a person who had not yet grown into her skin. I did not yet know who I was, and this must have appealed strongly to the MacIntosh desire to mould, to instruct, to control. As I look at old photographs, I can also see that I was attractive and smiling, and had a good figure. This apparently added up to something he was willing to fight for. At any rate, at the very moment of highest tension in the MacIntosh household, his bank transferred him to a small community in New Brunswick, 3,200 miles from his home in Alberta. We went downtown together that afternoon. He bought the licence, and I bought a white dress. The night before we boarded the train for our long journey east, we were married in the MacIntosh living room beside the needlepoint chair. His mother held a small stiff reception, and was gracious and smiling throughout, her eyes icy cold.

In the beginning, in our short freedom from responsibility, Thomas had known how to laugh and have fun. As long as he was fighting to possess me, he made me feel desirable, sought after, worthy. But almost from the moment he realized I was securely and irrevocably his, he started to examine me for flaws. Brainwashing always tells, and his mother's standards of behaviour and dress and speech were etched more deeply upon him than anything I could possibly provide. Besides, he was ambitious, and it was essential that I should not hinder his progress. He watched me carefully, and did not always like what he saw. This scrutiny hurt me long before it started to anger me, and by then the habit of silence was strong.

At first I felt that his criticisms were justified, and his newly acquired dignity impressed and intrigued me. I was young, and I was neither MacGregor nor MacIntosh. He was twenty-eight and an upwardly mobile bank employee. I could appreciate his desire to have me conform to his standards, which I assumed to be superior to mine. I felt branded by the Yukon and my father's blue collar. "If you please, Alfreda," Thomas would say, very cool, no fireworks. "Not that dress tonight. The Jamiesons know the most influential people in Woodstock. Wear your black. With the pearls I gave you for your birthday." I was still in love. If he had asked me to attend the party in a tiara, I might not have argued.

However, criticism, unless propped up by praise, impairs more often than it improves. According to him, I may have lacked class, a good background, advanced schooling, and discretion (one of his favourite words). I did not, however, lack intelligence. And ironically, the more he reproved and corrected me, the more I came to value my own upbringing and my own roots. After a time, I emerged from my blinkered condition. Suddenly one day, without warning, I looked around and said, out loud, "Who is this man I live with?" Once you have taken that first step, it is almost impossible to turn back.

I remember our first meal after asking that crucial question. I looked down at the end of the dining-room table and there, flanked by my two sons, was a Pekinese dog. And he was speaking.

"I know you will feel some pride, Alfreda," he said, coughing delicately into his fist, "when I tell you that the bank has seen fit to recognize my long years of service — useful and devoted ones, I might add."

I clasped my hands under the table. Why in heaven's name, I thought, does he always address me as though he were giving a speech to the Chamber of Commerce?

"That's nice, dear," I said.

"I am being transferred to Fredericton," he said, patting his mouth delicately with his napkin. "A very great honour. You will have the distinction, at long last, of being the wife of a manager of one of our nation's oldest banks. We move by the end of the month." He looked around the table, as though inviting applause.

Harold, age five, was already crying into his lamb chop. "Jimmy doesn't live in Fredericton," he sobbed. "I don't wanna live there. Please, Daddy. Tell them you won't go."

Young Thomas, mercifully nicknamed Tosh, was seven years old, and knew that a MacIntosh never cries. But his eyes were wide and bright, and his teeth were digging into his lower lip.

"Now, now, now, boys," purred Thomas Senior, scratching his vest, "congratulate your father. Fredericton is a much more impressive place in which to live than this small town. Why, it is the capital city of our province. And your father will be a very important man. This is cause for rejoicing, not for tears. Alfreda. Point out to your children the wisdom and honour of this move. And you, my dear, will certainly have to pull up your socks now that we are heading for high places."

I, who had been pulling up my socks for eleven years, saw no cause to rejoice. A familiar knot was forming somewhere just south of my rib cage.

"Congratulations, Thomas," I said.

❋

We moved into the bank manager's house on a foggy May day. The house was small, and the branch tiny. Nonetheless, one could tell by Thomas's posture, by the set of his chins, that he felt the top of the mountain was in sight.

"Why do you want this so much?" I asked him that evening

after the boys were in bed. "Why do you want so badly to be important, Thomas?" I had never before asked such a question, and I saw my hand shaking as I turned on the lamp by his chair.

"I consider that to be an impertinent and irrelevant question," he said, and rose stiffly to leave the room. Later, however, when the electric blanket was turned on and the lights were out, he said, "Mother always made it clear to me that I must aim for the top. She bought me educational toys. She scolded me if my marks were low. She pointed out that a MacIntosh must never take second place to anyone. She said that my father would agree, if he were living. She bought me books every Christmas, stories about great men. She said that this is what he would have chosen for me." He mumbled something.

"Pardon?" I asked.

I could barely hear him. "Every year I used to hope I'd get a teddy bear."

My heart lurched. Optimist that I was, I thought I was on the brink of meeting the real person who was my husband.

He continued. "And Alfreda," he said, once more addressing the Chamber of Commerce, "you will of course understand that you'll have to choose your friends with extreme care. A bank manager cannot be too cautious. You must realize that it is a position of enormous trust. We can't be entertaining just any old riffraff in this house."

I turned over to face the wall.

Five years passed, the boys grew older, and Thomas and I continued to live together and apart in the same house. Although he was watchful of me and critical of my shortcomings,

I'm sure that he looked upon himself as an excellent father and husband. In his own cool way, he probably loved us — if you can love people without making the slightest effort to know them. Once I said to him, "Thomas, I wish you'd have a talk with Tosh. He's twelve now, and seems awfully worried about something."

"Worried!" he exclaimed, clearing his throat, caressing his buttons. "Let him try for just one day to cope with *my* worries and he'd see how insignificant his own small troubles are. I'd like to watch him coping with fluctuating interest rates. You're the mother. Children are your territory. You speak to him. But no mollycoddling, mind! A MacIntosh must stand up to life without flinching."

A MacIntosh, indeed. After he left for work, I plunged my fist into a cushion, then threw it at the wall. I looked at the picture of his mother which stood on the mantel, and thought: Not one visit from that woman in fourteen years, and yet she is as present in this room as if she was sitting in that chair. I picked up another cushion and threw it at the chair. Then I went upstairs and cried for ten minutes. My tears were for all of us — for Tosh and his anxieties, for Harold and what was expected of him, for me and my new frustrations, for Thomas and the stranglehold his mother still had on him. Somewhere, I thought, somewhere inside of him there must be a real person, but whoever he is, he's locked in there too tightly ever to get out. I went downstairs to pick up the cushions and to vacuum the living-room carpet. We were having bank company for dinner that evening.

In May of that year I fell off a stool when I was spring-cleaning and broke my leg. For two whole months I was unable to keep the house as clean as a bank manager's house must be. So I engaged a cleaning lady to help me — a stout little woman called Geneva. She was originally from Saint John and was married to a sergeant at the nearby Gagetown base. She was about fifty-six, a hard worker and loquacious. The third week she was with us, she said to me, "I bin lookin' at that pitcher on the mantelpiece. I hate bein' nosy, but is the lady's name by any chance MacIntosh, same as yours?"

I said yes, it was.

"I knew her, then," she said, nodding her moon face, smiling, oddly excited. "Each week I bin lookin' at her and thinkin' I know her from somewheres, but she looked too old. All that white hair. But she was from my hometown. Eileen MacIntosh. I used to pass down her street on my way to school. That's how I come to be familiar with her. We wasn't born on the same side of the tracks." She gave a bitter little chuckle. "You'd know all about her early days, I guess." She looked at me warily.

I tried not to lie. "I never knew her father. She seemed to think he was an almost perfect man."

She snorted. "Perfect, eh? Well there's perfect and perfect. And if called upon to describe himself, that's for sure the word he would have used. His family were from Nova Scotia a long ways back, and there's no one so proud nor so stubborn as a Nova Scotian. Everybody knows that. And that's what the MacIntoshes was."

"MacGregors," I said.

She looked at me for a moment, and then produced a smile that was spare and smug. "No," she said, "MacIntoshes." And then went on. "He was as thin as a cadaver, and as tall as tall. Head like a hawk and back like a poker. He walked like he knew for certain that his first cousin on his mother's side was the King of England. Like someone was back there holdin' his train off the dirty sidewalks of Saint John."

I sat very still, hands clasped together to keep them from moving. I was afraid of stopping this amazing flow of information.

She looked at me slyly. "Want me to wipe down them walls now, Mrs. MacIntosh?"

"No, no, Geneva. Everyone needs a little break, and we're both tired, I'm sure. Just sit a minute and rest. The walls can wait." I hobbled over to the counter. "Let me get you a cup of coffee. Sugar?" I had some coffee waiting in a thermos.

"Three lumps," she said. "No milk."

We sat with our coffee cups, like two strangers. Any questions from me, I felt, would look too curious. Heart hammering, I sipped and waited.

Geneva was clearly torn between her enjoyment of the suspense and her eagerness to tell her tale. She took a few sips of her coffee and said, with maddening slowness, "Very good coffee, Mrs. MacIntosh."

"I hope it's not too strong," I said, stirring and stirring.

Finally she spoke. "They kept her hid, y'know, after it happened. They said she went away to college, but we knew different. Because the boy was from our part of town. Still and all, we was amazed that she took up with him. All that beauty and high class, sneakin' out at night to go dancin' and drivin' and whatever," and here she smirked, "with someone who had a round face and no taller 'n her. Mind, she was some tall. But he was reckless and fun, and everybody loved him; and I guess there wasn't much laughter and gaddin' about in that big house on Waterloo Street. You does some wild things when you're sixteen. It seems like you goes a little bit crazy for a time. If parents'd just sit back and let the fever pass over, oftentimes the madness'd just go away all by itself. But Mr. MacIntosh forbid her ever to so much as smile at Georgie. That's why all the pussyfootin' around after dark, I suppose."

"What about her mother?"

"Oh, her mother." Geneva sniffed. "Nice enough, I guess, and no snob like the old man. But no backbone. Whatever he said, that was th' law, and she never did stand up to him for one second. Obeyed him even when he wasn't around. I had all that from my cousin Sandra that did the cleanin' there for a while. She said Mrs. MacIntosh did a lotta cryin' and sobbin' behind her bedroom door, 'specially during them first long bad months. But I bet that mother wasn't what anyone would call an ounce of help to her girl. If one of your parents is sad all the time and the other one mad, there isn't much to choose from if you're lookin' for comfort."

"Sad," I said.

"Yes, siree." Geneva nodded. "She never left that house. We knew she wasn't in college because there was people who saw her pass by the window. If you're human and if you're young, you can't keep away from a window twenty-four hours a day. I seen her once myself towards the end of her time, face like an angel, because she was beautiful, y'know, and belly as round and big as an October pumpkin. And wistful in the face when she parted them curtains. And somethin' else, too. Angry."

She took a few swallows of coffee and delicately nibbled on a chocolate chip cookie, holding up the little finger of her small square hand. I waited, determined to say no more. Finally she put down her cup.

"The old man thought we was trash, and he woulda bin furious if he'd of known what we seen. We may of bin trash, but we wasn't blind. Nor was we deaf. There was times when you could hear that baby cryin' clear to the end of the block."

I was scarcely breathing. I put my cup and saucer on the end table; it rattled when I held it.

"But they wasn't there long," she continued. "After about a month, he musta shipped them both out, 'cause it was like she disappeared off the face of the earth. And sure as shootin' no one in that town ever saw her again. Not ever."

She put down her coffee and sighed, and was quiet for a few moments. Then: "Her father went around with his hawk head as high as ever, and his back as straight, makin' like nothin' had ever happened in that house to bring him down to the level of the rest of us. His blood was all mixed up with ours inside that baby's veins. That must of been some hard for him to take. But you'd never of known it to look at him."

She got up abruptly. "I'm real sorry, Mrs. MacIntosh," she said, "but all of a sudden I feel awful dizzy, and sick in the stomach or head or somethin'. I know I ain't done yet, but could I leave the rest of the work till Tuesday?"

She didn't wait for my answer, but put the vacuum and pail away, gathering up her coat and umbrella as quickly as she could.

At the door, I put my hand on her arm for a moment. "Geneva," I said, "I hope you'll be all right." We looked at one another for a long moment, and something passed between us. A kind of knowing. Then I broke the spell.

"I'd drive you home, but I'm expecting a visitor at twelve. I'm sorry."

She spoke once more. "From the pitcher, she looks for all the world like the old man. Still beautiful, though." She sighed again. "Don't look to me like she suffered much after all."

I just said, "Goodbye, Geneva." She turned without another word, and left. She never came to work for me again. She sent another woman in her place.

✳

I looked at Thomas at the end of the table that evening, rubbing his stomach, correcting the boys' table manners, delivering statements to me about bank policies. We were eating macaroni and cheese.

"This is something that my mother never served," he said, giving his plate a barely perceptible shove.

I looked at him and realized that the afternoon's revelations had not eased the prodding irritation that his arrogance always produced in me. For an hour or two that afternoon, Thomas had become something different to me. Even his mother had had new things to say as she looked out at me from the frame with her proud unlovable face.

But here I was reacting to them both in the usual manner. I watched him as he reduced Harold to tears with sharp criticisms of his speech, his work habits, his posture. "MacIntoshes don't cry," Thomas said.

Ah, but they do, I thought. What's more, Thomas, you would benefit enormously from a few tears yourself. And I could bring that about with one sentence. I smiled as I composed the four necessary words.

"Why are you smiling, Alfreda?" Thomas asked, puzzled, uneasy.

A fine household, I thought, when one is startled by a smile.

"Just thinking," I said. "Just thinking." Ashamed, I said no more. I thought of a dozen reasons to forgive, to excuse, to pity, to hold my tongue.

Then Tosh spoke. He sat up straight, and drew in his young chin in a familiar way. "Father," he said, "I'm getting extremely high marks in school. Is there no way you could send me to that private school — Rothesay, isn't it? — advertised in the

Gleaner? I know it costs a lot, but we're an important family, and I'd be associating with my own kind." He gave a little cough. "There'd be a better chance to realize my intellectual and social potential. It's not like you're a common labourer or anything."

I set my fork down very carefully and looked at my son. He looked unfamiliar, new. He's twelve years old, I thought. I hope it's not too late. Fear touched the back of my neck. Thomas was nodding, pursing his lips, patting, scratching, dabbing at his macaroni and cheese, looking with favour on his elder son.

***

It was not my intention to be cruel. After all, there were ways in which Thomas might find it a relief to know what I knew. I bought a miniature teddy bear the next day, and put it on his desk beside his calendar.

"Where did this come from?" he asked, after dinner.

"From me," I said. "It's a present."

"What an odd idea," he said, but he picked it up and stroked the fur with his index finger. Then he replaced it, changing its position several times, standing back to look at the effect.

I waited until after the national news. Then I brought him his favourite peppermint tea, brewed in the silver teapot, our wedding present from his mother.

"Thomas," I said, touching him gently on the shoulder. "If you have a moment, there are a few rather important things I'd like to discuss with you."

THE CANOE TRIP

WHEN CHARLES AND LUKE came to say goodbye, Susie was sitting in the rocker feeding the baby.

"Don't push him too hard, Charles," she said, almost shyly. "He's pretty little."

"You don't have to worry, Susie," he said. "You know that. I don't happen to think that pushing hard is what fathers are for."

Charles glanced at her fondly. She looks good feeding babies, he thought — or doing almost anything else, for that matter. But she was wearing that shapeless red dressing gown he hated. Why on earth, he wondered, does she choose to wear something that looks like an old gunny sack, when she could be showing off the marvellous body that she's got underneath? From time to time he suggested that she throw it away.

"I'll buy you another one," he'd beg. "For a non-birthday present. An expensive one. Blue. Blue would be nice. That soft stuff like velvet. I'd like that. You'd look gorgeous in it."

"Velour," she'd say. "No thanks, Charles. This one's comfortable. I feel like I'm crawling back into a warm womb. Besides, the colour cheers me up." She clung to it like a Linus blanket. And of course he didn't press it. He was not into nagging. That had been his father's territory. He felt a tension in his forehead and rubbed it, horizontally, with the fingers of his left hand.

Charles smiled down at his son. Luke looked like a carbon copy of himself — stocky and square, with an unmanageable mop of curly black hair. He was eight years old. The kid still had arms and legs that were shapeless and spindly, but Charles knew that in ten years he'd be built for moving pianos.

Dressed in a set of oilskins, Luke gazed up at his father from under his sou'wester with naked worship. They were dressed in identical suits — Luke's brand new and shining yellow, Charles's spotted and faded from a decade of canoe trips.

With some concern, Charles looked out the window at the steady drizzle; but the Bedford weather office had promised sun before eleven. The clock in the hall rang six o'clock. Only five more hours, maybe less. And it was clear from Luke's face that he wouldn't care if the heavens opened and poured forth locusts. This was his first canoe trip.

They'd been out in the canoe a number of times before — three times, maybe more. Charles had explained and demonstrated all the basic skills of paddling, and little by little, he had let Luke try out the different bow strokes. All had been harmony and pleasure. Charles had felt a dual reaction to all of this — pride in his own wise parenting, and an aching regret for those early expeditions with his father. As though it had happened an hour ago or yesterday, he could hear that exasperated voice.

"My God, Charles, surely you could have avoided that rock!"

"Keep your eyes open! The bowsman can't relax his vigilance for one second. You're paddling like a dreaming girl!"

"Tired? Don't be ridiculous, son! Being tired is part of the sport. Be a man!"

All he could remember about those early canoe trips was fear, arms like numb stumps, a smoking anger deep in his chest. Only when he finally went to Y Camp did he discover the pride and delight of canoeing. It took until then to realize that rivers wound through peaceful woods and flowered meadows, that birds sang above the water, that rabbits, squirrels, deer watched from the slippery banks.

Charles kissed the top of Susie's head, and touched the baby's cheek. "Your two men will be home by six, for sure," he said. "Maybe earlier. You can pick us up at Brown's Lake bridge, and we'll get my car tomorrow." He smiled at her. "Have a good day without us. There's a sale on at Eaton's. You might like to go. They're selling off . . . dressing gowns."

"It'll take more than bribery to get me out of this beloved garment," Susie said, pulling its soft warmth around her against the chill of the May morning. She smiled. "Have fun. Sure you've got the can opener? Matches?"

"Luke's in charge of both those things. Okay, son? Nothing forgotten or left behind?"

Luke pulled a crumpled piece of paper out of his pocket and studied it slowly, carefully. He grinned at his father. "All set. All systems go."

On the way to Smythe's Landing, Luke fell asleep, and Charles drove through the early morning with deep satisfaction. The soft drizzle intensified the lushness of the countryside. "My son and I," Charles whispered to himself. He visualized himself and Luke, year after year, setting out in companionable peace to explore the river systems, to ski the woods, to hike through miles of wilderness — bush crashing, travelling by compass, blazing trails. He saw them standing together beside quiet streams, casting flies into the water, reeling in fish after fish, cooperating in the business of landing and netting. And today was the launching.

An hour and a half later, as they drove down into the valley, Charles could see the grey river winding its way through the foggy woods. His chest knotted with excitement. When he finally reached Smythe's Landing, he slowed the car to a stop and poked Luke in the ribs. "Up and out, Luke," he said. "Pick up as much gear as you can, and put it down on the dock. I'll get the rest."

Still groggy with sleep, Luke started hauling stuff out of the car. Twice he dropped things. Three times he tripped over a stump or a branch. Once he fell.

Looks like me, Charles mused, but lacks my coordination. Takes after his mother, who can stumble over a feather. Lovable but clumsy — both of them.

However, Charles said nothing — as, indeed, he had carefully said nothing when Luke had dropped countless balls, failed to reach first base, lost minnow after minnow as he struggled to bait hooks, seemed unable to move with any kind of speed or grace. *Time. It just takes time. And patience.*

Today would be different. During Charles's description of the various paddling skills, Luke had shown remarkable understanding of the principles underlying the various strokes. And in the course of their few practice sessions on Maynard's Lake, he had done very well. He was also a willing and amiable helper. And intelligent.

"Dad."

"Yes."

"I'm wet. There's rain crawling down my neck."

"It's part of the sport, son. Pull down your hat and yank up your collar. Can't expect to be bone dry in a rain storm." The drizzle had increased to a full driving rain, and the canoe was slippery as they stowed their gear inside it.

"How many miles, Dad?" Luke asked as he adjusted himself in the bow.

"Just ten. A real short trip."

They pushed off. As the canoe moved smoothly out into the river, Charles experienced yet again the warm anticipation that attended the start of all canoe expeditions.

"Dad."

"Yes?"

"Can I change sides?"

"Not tired already?"

"Yes. Kind of. How much farther?"

"We've only gone a few hundred yards, Luke. We've got a long way to go. On my first canoe trip, my father and I went twenty-five miles."

There was a sound from the bow.

"What was that you said, son?"

"Nothing."

They rounded a bend, and Charles glimpsed a heron standing watch over the river on a submerged rock, silhouetted against the misty trees.

"Psst! Look!" Charles whispered.

"What, Dad?" Luke yelled. "I can't hear you."

Charles sighed as the startled heron left the rock and disappeared behind a group of spruce trees.

"Never mind. It's too late."

During the next hour, the rain increased. Charles scanned the sky in vain for some sort of opening in the cloud cover. So it was Luke who saw the mother duck and her four ducklings crossing the river. He turned around abruptly in his seat and waved his paddle, face wide open with joy.

"Hey! Look, Dad! Look!"

"Righto, Luke. Terrific. But listen. You can't leap around like that in a canoe. It's not a stable craft. They tip. Like *easily*. We could be in the water in nothing flat. Sorry, but that's just the way it is. Next time, just *tell* me."

They paddled on in silence. Every so often, Luke would point to something — a chipmunk, a beaver dam, an unusual flower, a rock that looked like a serpent. Charles mentioned things of beauty, of interest, of amusement. A perfect day, thought Charles.

"Dad."

"Yes?"

"Don't we ever stop?"

"Why? What do you mean, stop?"

"Like *stop*. You know. Stop paddling."

"But we're on a trip. Not a picnic. Wait till you're so tired you feel like you'll die if you do one more stroke."

"Dad."

"Yes?"

"That's how I feel."

Charles looked at his watch. And at the river bank.

"Look, Luke, there just isn't any place we can stop right now. There's a great spot further on where I'd planned to have lunch. Can you hang on till then? Maybe a couple of hours?"

Mutter from the bow.

"What?"

"Nothing."

My God, Charles thought, looking at the drenched figure in the bow, his small hands grasping the paddle — he's so little.

"Listen, Luke. Can you hear me?"

"Yeah."

"Stop paddling. I'll go it alone for a while."

"Okay, Dad."

"But look. Can you stop wiggling? Try to sit still."

"My foot's gone to sleep."

"Well listen, then. Try to ease down, and see if you can sit on the bottom of the canoe for a while."

Watching Luke ease down took stamina. He seemed to have at least four legs, and neither of his arms appeared to be performing any valuable function. Charles grabbed the sides of the canoe and stabilized it, as Luke maneuvered himself onto the bottom.

"Good. Now, rest."

Charles discovered that it was just as easy to paddle the canoe now as it had been when Luke had been helping. *Lily Dipper.* Charles heard this phrase from way back, twenty-five years ago: "Anyone who's got no more push on their paddle than that is nothing but a damn Lily Dipper." And "For God's sake, Charles, try to get a little more heft into your stroke!"

"Having fun, son?" He smiled at Luke.

"Sure. Great." He was hunched over, hugging himself.

"Cold?"

"A bit. It's okay."

Charles paddled on for the next hour. Would the rain never stop? He was sorry Luke was cold and wet, but by gosh, so was he. And the expedition was for Luke, after all. He was a patient and uncomplaining kid, but he wasn't exactly radiating rousing good cheer. Charles wondered if perhaps he wasn't demanding enough of him. Too hard was bad. But maybe too soft was worse.

"Up you get, son, and let's have some work out of you. I need your help."

"Sure, Dad. I'm fine now."

Charles had forgotten about the hazards of Luke moving around in a canoe. His blade, flattened on the water, just barely saved them from a spill, as Luke heaved his body from the floor onto the bow seat.

Another hour and it was time for lunch. Charles beached the canoe, and saw a tree where they might find some shelter. Then he hauled the heaviest knapsack out of the craft, while Luke laboured up and down the bank with smaller items. Water was pouring off their sou'westers and dripping off their noses.

"A good fire will take the chill out of our bones," Charles called out from the shore. "Get out the matches, while I get the bag of kindling and paper. We'll have the soup hot in no time."

When Charles reached the place he had picked out for lunch, he noted with satisfaction that it was almost dry. The pine tree was high and thick, and the ground was level and carpeted with pine needles. Then he saw Luke's face — white, bleak, *scared*.

"What's up, son? You'll be okay in a minute. Let's have the matches."

Luke just stood there dripping, motionless. Then: "They're not here," he said. "The bag's not here . . . That means the can opener, too."

"Luke." Charles spoke carefully. Mustn't spoil everything. "That stuff was your responsibility. I told you to pack it. And to check."

"I did pack it, Dad. And I checked it, too. The bag was in the car. But I don't even remember what I carried down to the canoe."

Charles's mind slid over the memory of Luke's sleepwalking exit from the car, stumbling, falling, eyes barely open. That hot soup was taking on all the appeal of a barbecued steak.

"We've got some bread and peanut butter, Luke," he said.

"No doubt we can survive on that." He could hear the edge in his voice.

Charles toyed with the idea of making a lark of their deprivation, of pretending to be pioneers surviving on pemmican. But then he thought, To hell with it. I'm too wet to care. Besides, it won't hurt him to find out that his errors won't always be greeted with a smile. Granted you can't build a man in a day, but you can start laying a few bricks. They ate their sandwiches in silence under the tree.

That afternoon they paddled three more hours. The rain stopped, but a stiff breeze came up from the north, and the going was hard. Charles struggled against the wind, while the Lily Dipper slogged along — in, out, in, out — without rhythm, out of phase, contributing nothing. Exhausted, Charles scraped his thumb against the side of the canoe, and he could see the blood starting to flow. Reaching forward to his knapsack, he dug into the front pocket for his first-aid kit. A Band-Aid wouldn't make it stop hurting, but it could keep him from spilling blood all over his gear. The kit wasn't there. It was inconceivable that it was not, but in the excitement of his departure, he must have forgotten to get it out of the car's front dash. It had been on his own list, carefully compiled with Luke's assistance. Maybe it had been Luke's job to get it. A part of him clung to this tempting idea.

He pulled a handkerchief out of his pocket and wound it around his thumb, tying it securely.

"You okay, Dad?"

"Yeah. Yeah, sure."

Sure. Wonderful. Wet, frozen to death, totally bushed, and to all intents and purposes, stark alone.

At last, mercifully, there was only about a quarter of a mile left to go. The sun had come bursting through the trees and the wind had died down. Just around that bend would be the bridge, where Susie would be waiting with a warm car and three dry daughters. Daughters. He could maybe try taking Colleen next time. She was big for her age, tough and spirited. There wasn't any law that said it had to be a *son* who went on canoe trips. He'd not had any sisters, and he still thought of little girls as made of sugar and spice, of material that lacked what his father used to call *fibre*.

Thunk! They hit a rock, and the canoe spun around.

The woods, the sky, the slithering river exploded with Charles's voice.

"Goddamnit, Luke! Didn't you see that rock? That's what a bowsman's *for*! You can't take your eyes off the water for one *second*! It's not like you're any damn use as a paddler. You could at least use your *eyes*! Am I supposed to do every goddamn thing myself?"

Luke swung around and stared at his father, eyes round, mouth open.

"Turn around, you little fool!" Charles yelled. "And see if just for once you can do it carefully. Try, just *try*, not to be so fucking clumsy! And *paddle*! There're rocks ahead, in case you didn't notice, and we have to get around them fast!"

Luke dug into the water with frenzied speed and zero control. His whole body was shaking, and the water splashed around his paddle as though he were throwing lumber into the river. Miraculously, they avoided the rapids, and Charles steered the canoe to a sandy beach, just their side of the bend. Beyond the point was the bridge and Susie's car full of daughters. He wasn't ready for them yet.

When the canoe came to a standstill by the beach, Luke sat like a statue, a small waxworks figure clad in yellow oilskins. Charles hung onto a tree that reached over the water; he leaned his forehead against the trunk and contemplated the empty cave that was the centre of his chest. Eight years of trying to be a perfect father, and in less than a minute, he'd blown the entire thing. He could see his father sitting on the river bank at the end of one of their canoe trips. He had been tall, lean, and immensely strong, and he was sitting on the grass with his head in his hands, tears streaming down his face. Charles had always assumed they'd been tears of anger and disappointment, after yet another frustrating trip — despair over a son who had failed once again to live up to his expectations.

As Charles sat there, gazing at his memory, he watched Luke drop his paddle in the river and fall out of the canoe.

They were close to the shore. There was no danger. Even the paddle was safe. But by the time he had fished Luke out of the water, laid him on the shore, and secured the canoe and the paddles, Charles's body was trembling like a poplar branch. Luke was sitting up on the wet grass, shivering, eyes staring straight ahead.

Charles stumbled back up the bank, and wrapped his own coat around Luke. Taking him in his arms, rocking him back and forth on his lap, like a baby, he moaned over and over again, "Oh my son, my son, my son."

After a long time, he stopped rocking, and both their bodies were still. Charles cleared his throat and said, "Are you okay, Luke?"

"Yes, Dad."

"Are you sure?"

"Yes." Then, "Are *you*?"

Charles closed his eyes. He didn't answer. Then he said, "That wasn't you I was yelling at back there, you know."

"No."

"Oh hell," Charles sighed. "I can't expect you to understand. How else can I put it?"

"But I do."

"Do what?"

"Understand. I did it last week." As he spoke, he fiddled with his father's shirt buttons.

"Did what?"

"What you just did. I got mad at Harvey because I was mad at something else. I yelled at him and threw a rock right through a basement window in that empty house on Hawthorne Street."

Harvey was Luke's best friend. Charles had never seen them exchange so much as a cross word.

"But when I'm with you, you're always so quiet and polite. How come?"

"Because that's the way you want me to be."

Charles passed his hands across his eyes. "You must have been pretty wild when you let fly at Harvey. What was the matter?"

"Oh, I dunno." Luke stopped fidgeting with the buttons and clasped his hands together in his lap. The sun was starting to dry his matted hair, his wet face.

"What? Tell me."

"Well . . ."

"C'mon Luke. Let's have it."

"Well. You. It was you I was mad at."

"Me! For what?"

"For yacking at Mom. You're all the time bugging her about that red dressing gown. I think it's really pretty. She looks cool in it. She likes it." He paused. "So I got mad."

Then Luke spoke again. "I'm sorry I spoiled your trip. I know you weren't yelling those awful things *really* at me, but I know I spoiled your trip."

My trip.

"You didn't, Luke. The weather did. *I* did. I should have planned a shorter trip. I should have let you practise more. I shouldn't have expected you to be eighteen years old. I'm the dumb one; not you. I don't know how to tell you this — how to fix it."

Luke stood up and grinned. "You don't have to," he said. "You just did." Charles held out his large brown hand, and Luke stretched out his thin arm. They shook hands. They looked at one another.

"I love you," Charles said.

"Me too, Dad," said Luke. "A whole lot."

Susie, the baby, and the two little girls were waiting at the bridge. As the car climbed the hill away from Brown's Lake, Charles turned around and looked down the steep hill.

"Look, Luke," he said.

In the distance the wet forest shone in the evening sun. The river was a dazzling ribbon of light moving through the valley below. A look of complete understanding passed between them.

On the way home, Luke talked for thirty minutes about the ducks, the beaver dams, the picnic in the rain, the hazardous rocks, the chipmunk. Then he fell asleep until they reached their house an hour later.

"Well," said Susie that night, as she and Charles prepared for bed. "Was it as great as you expected?"

Charles thought a moment before he answered. "Better," he said.

"Why? It was a pretty crummy day."

"Well, because among other things — among a whole lot of other things — it was the day I forgave my father."

"Oh?" She waited for more.

"Sometime I may tell you about it. Maybe. Maybe not."

Susie didn't press him. "Okay," she said. She was sitting at her dressing table in her slip, unfastening her earrings.

"One more thing," said Charles.

"What's that?"

"That red dressing gown . . ."

"Uh huh?"

"Keep it. Enjoy it." He grinned. "Money to buy a new one is from this moment withdrawn."

"Sometimes," muttered Susie, as she disappeared into the bathroom for her shower, "I don't even begin to understand men."

THE LOSERS

ARTHUR MACNAUGHTON THOUGHT of himself as a discriminating man. Therefore it pained him that James Harrison had suggested they meet for lunch in this particular restaurant. The sign above the door was in bold black letters, fashioned in some sort of shiny metal and placed uncompromisingly on a Kelly green background. As he approached the glass door, a haze of fingerprints obscured his view, but once inside the porch, the first thing to greet his critical eye was the cash register. "Cheap," he reflected, not entirely to himself. In fact, his lips moved, and a deaf person would have known exactly what he was saying.

Once seated in his booth (and booths, as his mother often commented, were vulgar), he surveyed with distaste the moulded red seats, the paper placemats, the menu encased in plastic. He drummed his fingers on the arborite tabletop, and waited for James.

James was someone he had never been able to understand. A physicist — a fact which made him immediately suspect — James had obviously risen to his present position from humble stock and meagre surroundings. He had been known to lecture in a mended sweater ("My favourite," he would say. "A comfortable old friend.") and to chew bubble gum when working on his research. Arthur had once entered his laboratory without knocking, only to be greeted by a grey-pink bubble the size of a tennis ball, behind which James's face was barely visible. And far from being disconcerted, James had laughed so hard that he'd had to bend over with a stitch in his side. "It's your face! It's your face!" he kept gasping. And just whose face, Arthur had wondered, are we discussing?

When Arthur had asked James if he really *meant* to meet at this restaurant (The Golden Spoon — better to have been named The Tin Spoon, The Greasy Spoon), James had looked hard at Arthur with the hint of a grin flickering at the corners of his mouth. What the devil could he possibly find amusing in such a query, and why didn't he reply? But James had finally answered.

"Yes," he said. "Because the parking lot is always full of trucks."

"Of trucks? James . . ."

"And if there's a fleet of trucks outside a restaurant, the food inside is always good. Without fail. No quiche, mind you. But good."

Well, Arthur hadn't argued further. If the vice president (academic) — physicist notwithstanding — wants to meet you for lunch, you go. And you go to the place of his choosing. With tenure what it is today, a wise man doesn't balk at matters of taste.

Arthur frowned. James was late. Taste was one thing. Punctuality was another. His mother had made that abundantly clear. That was one of her favourite phrases: *abundantly clear*. And she seemed forever to be sitting heavily on his left shoulder, judging. He felt a moment of confusion as he tried to sort out who was the source of his irritation this time, James or his mother.

Across the restaurant from Arthur, just out of earshot but in full view of his booth, a man and a woman were eating their lunch. He looked at them carefully, assessing their worth. "Don't stare," he could hear his mother saying. He sighed. Feeling a fullness in his throat, he placed a finger inside his starched collar, moving it around at the front of his thin neck. Loose enough. Probably just some kind of spasm.

The couple on the other side of the room were deeply engrossed in one another's company. Arthur marvelled that this should be the case. It was true that the man's suit was impeccable and his tie well chosen. But his face was unattractive in the extreme. Formless and puffy, his cheeks almost obscured a pair of beady little eyes. His mouth was large and loose, his nose small and flat. But when he smiled, which was often, his smile was wide and delighted.

Delighted by what? Arthur wondered, switching his scrutiny to the man's partner, visible only from the side. She was, he felt, a fitting luncheon companion for such a man. He could hear his mother's pronouncement when faced with a couple she found unpleasing: "A pity," she would say, "to spoil two houses."

And what, Arthur asked himself, could this man find to smile about while dining — no, eating — with this unfortunate young woman? Blatantly gaptoothed and chinless, she looked out at the world and her lunch companion from behind the thickest pair of glasses that Arthur had ever seen. But it was her hands that upset him most. Small and formless, they flapped around her as she spoke, in a manner that he found affectedly feminine. When she picked up her cup, not one but three of her fingers stood up in a curved little fan. The skin on her hands was a milky bloodless white; they looked as though they lacked bones or even muscles. They were like two invertebrate fish. He couldn't imagine them able to hold a pen, a trowel, a mixing spoon. He imagined her striking a typewriter key, only to have her finger collapse under the stress of the blow. In terrible fascination he watched those small flaccid fingers waving above her omelet (the only thing she'd have the strength to cut, he felt), and marked the naked pleasure she was taking in her friend's company.

Ah! Arthur's eyes widened. He suddenly understood everything. When you have nothing, when you *are* nothing, not only are you resigned to imperfection, you probably crave it. These two sad people had been passed over by Nature's paintbrush (Arthur nodded with appreciation of this phrase), but they found solace and relief in each other's company. Such a pair could even conceivably be . . . married. "The poor," his mother said from his left shoulder, "are always satisfied with less." A pity, indeed, to spoil two houses.

"Arthur," said James's familiar lazy voice. "I'm sorry to keep you waiting. I was waylaid by a hysterical and pregnant student."

Arthur wanted to ask who was more important — he, Arthur MacNaughton, talented (although unpublished) author, or some obscure student who hadn't had the sense to protect her virginity. But he thought about tenure and held his peace.

James took off his coat and revealed his mended sweater. "Try the beefsteak and kidney pie," he said. "Afterwards go back to your office and write a poem about it." Then he said, "Arthur."

"Yes." Arthur could feel his shoulders tighten. "Yes?"

"You'll get your letter in the mail tomorrow," James said,

giving Arthur his full attention, "but you and I are old friends from a long way back. I just wanted to say in person how pleased I am."

Arthur cleared his throat. "Pleased?"

"Yes." James smiled. "Tenure. You've got it."

Arthur could hear a sigh — certainly of relief — and he didn't know if it was his own or his mother's. But before he could even say thank you, James chuckled quietly.

"Well!" he said. "It seems we have chosen our restaurant wisely. We're certainly in good company. We're dining — more or less — with tomorrow's honorary graduands. Fall Convocation can often be a bit of a fizzle, but never have we handed out honorary degrees to two more distinguished people."

Arthur raised his head slowly and followed the direction of James's gaze. Could it really be so? It could. There sat his terrible couple, symbols of the world's losers. Dame Abigail Rochester, internationally famous sculptress, who had created that magnificent stone carving outside the Arts Building; and Joseph Windsor, last year's winner of the Pulitzer Prize — possibly Arthur's favourite author.

Finding his hands were shaking, he put down the plastic menu and locked his fingers together on his lap. He longed to speak to his mother, but she had been dead for five years. He wanted to say something final and angry to her. Like: "*So there!*" Something like that.

But suddenly Abigail Rochester and Joseph Windsor were beside the table, shaking James's hand. At ease, as always, James said, "I'd like you to meet one of our own respected writers, Arthur MacNaughton." Arthur rose hastily, knocking over the salt cellar, crumpling his paper napkin into a damp ball. "I'm delighted," he said, "to meet both of you." Taking Abigail Rochester's hand in his, he felt the strength of her grip and the steadiness of her gaze through those thick glasses. Her eyes were brown and warm. The skin of her hand felt like Indian silk. He wanted to rub his thumb over it, back and forth, back and forth. Turning to Joseph Windsor, he said, "I admire your work tremendously," and watched as the man's swollen face was transformed by that radiant smile.

When Arthur sat down, when he and James were alone again, he found that his hands were no longer shaking. He was quiet for a while, staring out the window.

"Well?" James said, after a few moments.

Arthur took a deep breath. Without realizing he was doing it, he loosened his tie and undid the top button of his shirt. He looked at James and smiled; . . . *old friends from a long way back . . . one of our own respected writers.* "I think I'd like to try the beefsteak and kidney pie," he said. His shoulders felt remarkably relaxed. Almost, he thought, weightless.

THE DRESS

"ALL MY EMOTIONAL SEAMS are unravelling," Clarissa had said to Sybil at suppertime on June 3, when she dropped by to borrow a cup of flour. Sybil could hardly wait to get herself over to Martha Hennigar's the following day to tell her.

"Sybil Trueman!" Martha said. "You have to be kidding! No, on second thought, you don't. Anyone else in the world would say that they were feeling nervous. But not our Clarissa. No siree. *Her* emotional *seams* are unravelling."

It was enough to put life into a hot morning. Martha had been sitting, wilted, beside the wading pool in her spacious back garden, watching her four children jump, fall, or be pushed into their large plastic pool, $12.98 at the latest K mart sale. A bargain. Martha looked at it with satisfaction, her mind straying momentarily from Clarissa and her unravelling seams. Large, she mused. Wet, safe, cool . . . and cheap. Her thoughts played briefly with the idea of immersing herself in the pool for just a few short refreshing moments. But this was not her way — to give in to anything like heat, or illness, or toothache, or visiting in-laws.

"I'm tired of Clarissa's nerves," she said suddenly. "She only has two children. Just The Lump . . ."

"You mean Shirley?"

"Yes, Shirley. And Martin. Hardly enough to make life a burden. She should try four. All under six. And lively. Unlike Shirley, who as far as I can tell, just sits. Gloomily. No chasing up and down Charles Street after our Shirley. No, indeed. Stuff her six-year-old-mouth with cookies and she'll sit like a stone and just watch you. Unravelled seams, indeed!"

Sybil could manage to look cool, even on a day like this. But she wiped her cheeks under her dark glasses with a surreptitious index finger. The heat was settling in. Eleven o'clock, and already the air had a steamy substance to it. Heavy, tangible, pressing on her head. Over in the park, two blocks away, you could hear children screaming — with delight, Sybil assumed wryly, her three sons being in the park at that very moment. And thank heavens that's where they are, she thought, or on a day like this my own seams could undo a bit.

"She caters to that child," Sybil said, after a long silence.

"Who?" Martha asked. She was disentangling her son's foot from a red plastic bucket.

"The Lump."

"Oh yes. Couldn't agree more. Hovers over her like a phantom, twitching. Concerned about the condition of her psyche. Feeling every blow that comes her way. Look at that pudding face just once and you can tell that her life is going to be one blow after another."

"Well," Sybil hesitated, fishing for words, "she has a kind of sweetness about her."

"*Who?*"

"The Lump."

"My God, Sybil. I'd as soon assign sweetness to an oatmeal muffin. If spineless is sweet, she's sweet."

Martha fished into a canvas bag for her cigarettes. She took one out, but it stuck to her fingers, then to her lips, and she put it away. "Harry!" she called to the centre of the garden, "Stop pulling Laura Lee's hair! And Laura Lee, stop that ridiculous shrieking!" Frowning, she turned to Sybil. "If you turn your head for one second, they try to murder each other."

"Well," began Sybil, "I do feel they have to work it out somehow."

"Work out what?"

"Murderous instincts. Aggression. Healthy competitive urges. When my boys start fighting, I plug in my Walkman and paint my fingernails, or else vacuum the carpets. I figure by the time they reach manhood, they'll emerge as civilized people. Nine times out of ten it happens that way. Look at that charming Mr. Strathroy in our church. They say he was a terror as a youngster, and now, there he is taking up the collection at St. John's and smiling at the congregation."

"At the ladies, anyway, or so I've heard."

"Oh come on now, Martha. Live and let live is what I say. Anyway, Mr. Strathroy has charm, and if my boys end up charming, I'll be satisfied. I've got better things to do with my time than be a policeman."

Martha pursed her lips. Her main feeling about Sybil's sons at the moment was joy that they were in the park instead of in the Hennigar backyard. If there was one thing she didn't need on a hot day, it was the three Trueman anarchists. If she had to hear Sybil say "Boys will be boys" one single time today, she might spit right into the wading pool. "Janet," she yelled. "Leave the baby *alone!*"

"Clarissa doesn't approve of yelling at her kids," Sybil said. "Myself, I think it's healthy."

"Myself, I think it's necessary, unless you want your home to be another Flanders Fields."

There was silence under the beach umbrella while Martha fanned herself with the *Globe and Mail*. Sybil continued to wipe perspiration off her face with the tips of her fingers. She watched absently as Laura Lee pinched Julian, the youngest Hennigar. Strapped into his stroller, he started to cry. "Dear heavens," muttered Martha as she strode out to rescue him. "Right now I'd sell all of my four in exchange for one Lump. Psyche be damned. I'd like a little peace." But by the time she had soothed Julian, Janet was crying because Harry had thrown her doll into the wading pool.

A pale face appeared from behind the privet hedge, peering. "May we be permitted to enter?" it asked.

May we be permitted to enter. Martha sighed. "Yes, of course. Come on in. Welcome to the jungle. It's just us here, and the kids."

"Hi, Clarissa," Sybil said. "How are things?"

"Well, okay, I guess." Clarissa brushed a strand of hair from her damp face with limp fingers. "Hiram has taken Martin off to Ontario Place and this has left Shirley and me alone at the ranch."

"How come he didn't take Shirley, too?" asked Martha.

"Oh well." Clarissa hesitated. "You know Hiram. Likes to terrify Martin on all the rides. Said Shirley might cry or be sick or something. He's not renowned for his patience."

And who would be? "Pretty hot, eh?" Sybil offered.

"Oh my, yes," breathed Clarissa. "And I seem to be feeling so unhinged of late. It rather alarms me."

"Well, don't be scared." Martha frowned. "Unhinged isn't

all that special, you know. I'm not feeling particularly hinged myself this afternoon. Four kids keep you hopping." *Unlike two.*

"The Lump is here! The Lump is here!" chanted Laura Lee, her golden curls bobbing up and down as she danced between the lilac bushes.

"Stop that!" Martha shouted. "Now just *stop!*"

Clarissa's long face was bleak.

"Oh, let them be!" Sybil sighed, crossing her slender legs. "They'll work it out." Clarissa's appearance, she was thinking, is not improved by those worry marks between her eyebrows; and she shouldn't wear her hair so long. Not when it's so thin. Not when she's forty. Not in a heat wave. Sybil ran her fingers across her own smooth brow, and patted her hair, feeling its bounce.

"How are the plans for the birthday party tomorrow?" Martha asked.

"Well," Clarissa began uncertainly, "I'm always crushed by anxiety, of course, in case I've left anyone out. One doesn't want to trammel any young spirits through want of an invitation. And Martin, of course, feels excluded and fragile because it's not *his* birthday. And I'm so afraid that Shirley won't *participate.* Although she's particularly happy today."

Watching the dumpy little figure standing on the fringes of the group of children, Martha thought, If this is happy, I'd hate to see sad.

Clarissa continued. "The favours are okay. Or at least I *hope* they are. And we're having hot dogs. No one seems to be allergic to them, unless they're upset by the nitrates. My goodness, but I'm hot."

"We're *all* hot," Martha said.

Suddenly Shirley approached the women and announced, "I have a beautiful new dress!" Shirley was not given to speaking unless spoken to. Her mud-pie features were transformed by joy.

"Yes!" Clarissa said, beaming. "We finally found a dress. I thought I would expire of heat and frustration all week. Dress after dress after dress, and all of them simply dreadful. Then suddenly — a miracle. She looks so beautiful in it." She fished in her shopping bag. "We just got it this morning. *Look!*"

The dress was pale pink, with tiny rosebuds embroidered on the material. Cut simply, it fell from a wide yoke, with a little stand-up eyelet collar in white. She held it up to Shirley, whose face radiated delight. The pink brought out the deep brown of her enormous eyes, making the onlooker forget her large nose, her weak chin. The worry lines had disappeared from around Clarissa's face. "Oh Shirley," she said, hugging the fat little girl, "I do love you so very very much."

Martha watched this display of affection, and then looked at Laura Lee. The same age as Shirley, Laura Lee was slender, dainty, aggressive, confident, pretty. A winner.

Then Shirley returned to her position ten feet from the pool.

"I worry about her so," sighed Clarissa.

"Who?" Martha asked, knowing exactly who.

"Shirley. She's so afraid of everything. Heights, dogs, water, strangers. Things like that. Hiram took her in hand and tried to fix things awhile back, but when it didn't work, he gave up."

"Like how?" Sybil asked.

"Oh, you know. 'Grasp the nettles,' he would say to her, 'and they won't hurt you.' Took her out to see those guard dogs at Peterson's Corners. Threw her off the end of the wharf at the cottage. He said she'd swim before she'd drown. Claimed it was a proven method. I, of course, was beside myself with fear, but he was right. She didn't drown. She swam ashore."

"And then what?" Sybil was leaning forward. "It sounds like such a great idea."

"She climbed onto the dock and walked right into the cottage, without looking at either of us. I wanted to follow her, but Hiram said no. 'Let her absorb her triumph in peace,' he said. Later I found her curled up in a ball on her bed, eyes wide open, as though she was afraid to close them."

"But the water," Sybil prompted, "what about her fear of the water?"

"Oh, that." Clarissa sighed again. "She won't even step on the dock. And when we go to Lake Huron, she stays up on the sand dunes, a good thirty-five feet from the water's edge."

"And Hiram?"

"Pretends she isn't there. He can't bear a coward. Says he was afraid of things when he was a child, and he claims it wrecked his fun. So he's determined to have brave children. Hence Ontario Place and the Ferris wheel and the Whip. He may have given up on Shirley, but he's resolved to make a hero out of Martin."

"Time for a cool drink," Martha announced, and disappeared into the kitchen. Returning with a tray of lemonade, she set it down on the table and ran her fingers through her damp hair. "We're going downtown this afternoon to get Laura Lee a new dress for the party. Nothing fits her this summer. She's got so big. Just look at her."

Even before she said it, Martha knew she shouldn't be talking about Laura Lee's size to Clarissa. She must look like a fairy to her, Martha thought, surveying The Lump with guilty satisfaction.

Clarissa stayed just long enough for a drink of lemonade. The hand that reached for the glass was trembling. Shirley was sitting on the grass, shoulders hunched, watching the other children playing. There was a small sad sweet smile on her lips, and her eyes were filled with longing.

✳

That afternoon, Martha and Sybil, with Laura Lee in tow, set off for the mall. Even on a hot day, shopping can seem like a holiday, if six children are left behind. Martha had got a sitter for her three, but Sybil felt she didn't need to leave anyone with the boys. "The park's supervised," she said. "Anyway, they're okay. You have to teach them self-reliance. Chuck and I agree on that."

Martha declined comment. The woman lacks imagination, she thought. What if one of the boys breaks an arm or something?

Finally — "What if one of them breaks an arm or something?" she asked.

Sybil turned to her, amazed. "Breaks an *arm*? Who on earth is going to *break an arm*?"

Oh well. Better Sybil than Clarissa — Cassandra, forever dreaming up broken arms.

The mall was predictably hot and crowded when they arrived. But not hotter, Martha pointed out, than her own backyard. Heads turned to look at Laura Lee a second time as she passed, her pert face shining with anticipation, her small feet striding along beside the two women. But the holiday spirit waned as they tried on more and more dresses in the hot cubicles. Most of them fit well and looked pretty, but there were almost too many to choose from, and Laura Lee didn't seem wholly satisfied with any of them. Martha could feel her patience running thin. As far as she could see, the very first dress they had tried on would have been perfect. Then, just as they were leaving Eaton's, Laura Lee stopped and pointed.

"That one! Oh Mummy! Look in the window! That's the one! It's *eggzactly* what I want!"

"Oh no!" Martha wailed, surveying a dress identical to Shirley's. "I'm sorry, darling, but that happens to be the one dress in the whole mall that you can't have. It's the same as Shirley's."

"Oh!" Laura Lee was devastated. "Oh *Mummy!*" An odd smile touched her face and was gone. "Mummy," she said, looking her sweetest, smiling her prettiest, "can't we try it on, just to *see*? Please. Just let me try it on."

"Go on," Sybil sighed. "Why fight it? It'll only take five minutes."

Five minutes later, Laura Lee stood in front of the mirror, the dress on. Below her beautiful little face, the lace collar stood up like a frame. On her delicate figure, the simple lines of the dress, the tiny rosebuds in the material, were a delight. Martha felt a stab of sadness, and then a nudge of anger. *If it wasn't for The Lump, my Laura Lee could have this dress.*

"A doll!" the saleslady gasped. "A little princess! Well, Mother, I can certainly see that we have to have *this* dress!"

"Oh for Pete's sake, Martha, take it," Sybil said, sitting down on the chair outside the door. "Like Hiram says, the kid has got to learn about life. It won't be the first time she turns up at a party in the same dress as somebody else. She'll recover. Probably do her good."

"But it's *her* party, and the dress is so special."

"Exactly. It's her party, and she'll be getting lots of attention and presents, and she doesn't *need* the dress. Besides, any goofball can see that the dress is special to Laura Lee, too."

Laura Lee twirled around twice and looked at herself over her shoulder.

"No," Martha said. "I just can't do that. Sorry, Laura Lee,

but we'll have to find something else." She sighed. "There are lots and lots of pretty dresses."

But it seemed that this was not so. The light had dimmed in Laura Lee's eyes, and her shoulders sagged as she tried on dress after damp dress. The colour was wrong, the material itched, the buttons were too tight, the frills were too deep.

"I don't remember caring this much about clothes when I was six," Martha said, wiping her brow, her nose, her neck.

"You didn't play with Barbie Dolls from the time you could open your eyes," Sybil said. "Thank heavens I have boys."

"Yes, I did so play with Barbie Dolls," said Martha. "I'm younger than you. It's mine she plays with."

"Well anyway, I think it's all stupid. The pink dress is perfect, she loves it, we all think she looks like an angel in it, and probably three other kids will turn up at the party in it, too. Have you thought of *that*? *Then* you'll feel pretty silly. I'm hungry. Let's go home."

That's true, Martha thought. The dress is featured in the front window. I'll bet you anything that Susie Johnston's mother will snap one up if she sees it. And Sybil is right, in a way. Turning up in someone else's dress is just another part of life to be learned. Maybe it'd make it easier for her next time. Besides, Shirley seemed so pleased with that dress, so lit up about it, that she may not even care. And the party is tomorrow. We haven't time to search through every darn store in town.

"Okay, Laura Lee," she said. "It's yours."

❋

The next day was rainy and cold. What a strange climate, Martha thought, staring out the window at limp lilacs, tulips bent under the driving rain, people hugging themselves as they raced up the street. But there was no time now for contemplation of the weather. She had to prepare lunch, wrap Shirley's present, make a couple of essential phone calls, bath the baby, pick up the sitter, and dress herself and Laura Lee — all in the next two hours. Hurriedly she started to cut bread for sandwiches.

At half past one, Martha was almost ready. Sybil was to call for her at 1:50, with George, her youngest and wildest. She shook her head, marvelling at the blindness of some otherwise intelligent parents when faced with the task of rearing children.

"Stop that, Laura Lee!" she called into the family room. "You leave that baby alone! One more time and I won't take you to the party!"

Laura Lee pinched the baby's leg.

"Laura Lee! You heard me! Now get yourself upstairs and take your clothes off. I'll come up and help you with your dress in five minutes."

But when Martha reached Laura Lee's room ten minutes later, the dress was already on. Laura Lee was standing in front of the mirror in frank admiration of what she saw — white socks bright against her tanned legs, patent leather shoes shining, clean hair, bouncy and golden. She turned this way and that, a soft closed smile on her face. She had never looked prettier.

Martha felt a stab of something she was too rushed or too unwilling to identify.

"Good for you!" she said. "I'll just be a second or two changing my clothes, and then I'll be ready."

At 2:15, late as usual, Sybil honked the horn as she drew up beside the Hennigar house. Swathed in raincoats and kerchiefs, Martha and Laura Lee dashed out to the car.

"You'd better both come in the front seat with me," Sybil

said, holding open the door. "Two kids plus one back seat equals instant mayhem." Sybil herself looked perfectly groomed, calm, untouched. They drove to Clarissa's house with George kicking the front seat, nonstop, as hard as he could.

As they stopped in front of the gracious white house on the corner of Simcoe and Main Streets, it was clear that the party was already in full and noisy swing. Through the picture window they could see balloons flying; music, giggles, shrieks issued forth from the screen door. Shirley was laughing, actually laughing, when they rang the doorbell, and she flew to open it. Brown eyes shining, face aglow with joy, she stood resplendent in her new dress, smoothing the folds of material over her fat stomach. Behind her stood Clarissa, all anxiety erased from her face. Maternal delight, relief, and, yes, pride, radiated from her thin features.

"Come in! Come in!" she cried. "We're in the middle of our first game of Musical Chairs. Oh, Martha! Sybil! It's all going so beautifully! Even Hiram is pleased."

Shirley happily surveyed her two new guests as they unbuttoned their coats. Martha felt a hot lump of fear settle into her chest as she searched the room for Susie Johnston. Yes, there she was. But no, her mother had not discovered the darling dress in Eaton's window. No little girl in the room, in fact, was wearing a dress half as pretty.

Shirley fingered the lace at her throat, as George dropped his wet coat on the floor and raced into the living room. Laura Lee was taking her time. Like a fashion-show model slowly displaying her wares, she spread her coat wide open, and then, with remarkable grace, slipped it off her shoulders and onto her right arm. "Here," she said, handing it to Clarissa with her small tight-lipped smile. The children who had come out to watch the arrival let out a communal "*Ohhhh!*" at the sight of her. They might hate her for her beauty ten years from now, but this afternoon, at six years of age, they loved her for it. Like a duchess, she sailed into the living room.

Martha dared to look at Shirley. She stood there not moving, holding her present. Gone was the radiance, all the hot glow, and with it all semblance of attractiveness. The Lump had returned, and the pudgy features no longer had anything to offer. Martha's breathing felt constricted.

"Clarissa," she pleaded. "Listen. I was sure you wouldn't mind. We knew there'd be lots of presents for Shirley. And Laura Lee loved it so. And it was late. And hot."

But Clarissa didn't answer. She was staring at her with a gaze of such unreadable intensity that Martha had to look away.

"Come in, my darling," Clarissa whispered fiercely, "and play games at your lovely party." Her hands were on Shirley's shoulders, the knuckles white.

But Shirley did not speak. Slithering out from under her mother's hold, she walked slowly into the kitchen, shoulders hunched. Sitting down on the kitchen stool, her hands limp in her lap, she let the tears slide down her heavy face.

Hiram chose this moment to emerge from the living room, rubbing his hands together jovially. "Well, well, well now!" he roared. "Welcome to our party! Where's the birthday girl? In you come, my dear, and be a good hostess . . . What . . . Well, *shit*! Clarissa! Get the kid off that stool and into the living room!"

With amazing speed, Shirley slipped off the stool and raced upstairs to her room. At first Clarissa did not move. She just stood there, staring at Martha. Finally, she opened her hand and let Laura Lee's raincoat slide to the floor. Then slowly, as though in a trance, her arms hanging at her sides, she moved up the stairs, past Shirley's room, past the bathroom and the linen closet, and into her own bedroom, closing the door behind her.

"I'll go see about Shirley," Martha said, and ran up the stairs to her room. There she found her lying in a tight ball, eyes wide open. "Oh my God!" breathed Martha and raced down again.

"Listen, Hiram," she said, as she reached the bottom of the stairs. "Kids at parties don't notice anything that's going on except the games and the food and the favours. Forget Clarissa and Shirley right now. We haven't time to get upset about them. I'll help you with the games. And Sybil — you get the hell out to the kitchen and start cooking those hot dogs. Hiram. Go in there and keep smiling." Martha herself marched into the room clapping her hands and shouting gaily, "C'mon now kids! Everybody up for the last game of Pass the Orange before we start the scavenger hunt."

It was during the cartoon video that she started noticing the sounds. The children were making so much noise that none of them could hear. Martha could, though. And Hiram. Above them, coming from the direction of Clarissa's bedroom they heard loud unmuffled sobs which periodically gave way to a keening wail that seemed to contain all the sorrow in the world. Like the howl of a coyote, Martha thought, or the call of a loon. And there were thumping noises that Martha did not want to identify. Hiram left the living room and rushed upstairs. Martha turned up the stereo to top volume and closed the living room door when she saw Hiram leading Clarissa downstairs. No one noticed their departure in the car.

Martha and Sybil stayed until Hiram came back from the hospital. By then, the dishes were washed, the presents piled in a corner of the sofa, the streamers removed, the table reset for supper. Hiram sat down on the sofa and put his head in his hands. His voice was muffled.

"What in God's name could trigger a thing like that?" Looking up at Martha and Sybil, he said warmly, "You've been so enormously kind. I'll never be able to thank you enough. Where's Shirley?"

"Hiram," Martha said carefully. "She's upstairs on her bed. I'm not a good one to give advice, but . . . go easy on her. She's had a shock. Try the velvet glove, eh?"

"What on earth kind of shock?" Hiram asked.

"She'll probably tell you," said Martha, "in which case I think I'll just be running along. I'm sorry. Goodbye, Hiram."

*

"Lookit, Martha," Sybil said, as soon as they got in the car. "Don't blame yourself. Besides, what's a dress, anyway? A *dress*! Lordy but I'm glad I don't have any girls. Perk up, Martha. The sky hasn't fallen."

Martha looked at Sybil's face — serene, composed. "That's where you're wrong, my girl. The sky has most definitely fallen. And it's all our fault."

"*Our* fault! Well, that I *do* object to."

"You urged me. I didn't want to. You gave me all the reasons why I should buy it. You said you were hungry and wanted to go home."

"Well for God's sake, Martha. You're a free agent. You didn't have to listen. *You're* the one that *bought* it."

Martha sighed. She felt angry at so many people that it was hard to untangle the anger. At Clarissa for falling apart. For letting her seams unravel totally, in fact. At Shirley for being unattractive. At Laura Lee who was sitting up looking so pleased, so smug, so removed from pain. At George, who was still kicking the front seat. At Sybil for tempting her. At herself. Oh, at herself.

"Goodbye," she said as Sybil dropped them off at the Hennigar house.

"Perk up, doll," Sybil called. "It's not worth worrying about. Nothing is." She looked in the rear view mirror, adjusted her neck scarf, and was gone.

✳

That evening, after Laura Lee was in bed, Martha took the dress and sat down, holding it for a while in her lap. Finally, she took it over to the box that she kept open for contributions to her cousin Mark's Harriet. Mark was on Unemployment Insurance, and Harriet was six. But she didn't put it in. She went upstairs and almost dropped it into the green garbage bag that held articles for the Goodwill outlet. Standing for a time in the middle of the room, she held the dress in her hand. Then, moving quickly, she went up to the attic and chose a box from a pile that she saved for Christmas wrappings. Placing the dress in the box, she taped it shut and went down to the family room. Kneeling down, she lit the fire, which was already laid, and when it was burning strongly, she placed the box on top of the logs.

At first, nothing happened. The box was a sturdy one, and for a while it just sat there on top of the flames. Then, slowly, a thin ribbon of smoke curled out of the corner of the box, growing to a thick stream. Finally the flames licked up the side, and the fire took hold.

"What on earth are you doing?" her husband asked as he entered the room. "I smelled something strange. What is it?"

"Laura Lee's dress," Martha said. "I'm burning it."

"You're *what*?"

"Burning it. I know. It doesn't make sense. But it's something I just have to do."

"But *why?* Sure, you feel badly about what happened, but good grief, it cost forty-five dollars."

"I know. I'll pay for it out of my Avon money."

"But it's such a *waste*. Someone could *use* it. It just seems so *stupid*."

"I agree, Jake." Martha frowned. "I can't explain. Just bear with me, if you can. I know it's a waste. So were burnt offerings. And no one questioned their validity."

He watched her for a long moment.

"Okay, honey," he said, giving her sagging shoulders a little pat. He looked at her with concern. "I'm upstairs in the den if you need me."

Martha stayed there on the floor of the family room, just as she was, until the last particles of the box and the dress were ashes. Then she rose wearily, put the screen in front of the fireplace, and went quietly to bed.

JANETTA'S CONFINEMENT

SHE WAS SEVEN and a half years old, and tall for her age. Her hair was no-colour beige, and it hung down, lank and straight, from two hot-pink bunny barrettes. Her face was not striking in either its beauty or its ugliness. No one, in fact, could have predicted how its features would eventually arrange them-selves. Puberty was still far off; she had a straight-up-and-down body, legs like posts, long formless fingers.

Her name was Janetta — apparently the only remarkable thing about her. Sometimes she would write her name on a piece of paper, wait until the ink dried, and then run her index finger across it, stroking, stroking. Other times, she would lock the bathroom door and study herself in the mirror — this way, that way, over her shoulder, straight on. She could make nothing of that face. She came to no conclusions. Then, three weeks might pass before she would look at herself again — *really* look, that is. She would examine her face to make sure that bubble gum wasn't sticking to her chin, or in order to pick her teeth after eating corn on the cob, but that was mainly because her teeth felt tight and uncomfortable. And to check if her barrettes were aligned.

Once she had seen Judy Merino downtown in Scotia Square. Judy was from school, in Grade Three. She was looking at a display of neon T-shirts — fiery pink, blazing mauve, electric blue, glaring yellow. She was holding them up under her chin, one colour at a time, in front of the mirror, taking a long careful moment to study the effect of each one. On her hair, one purple barrette was firmly fastened beside the upper right-hand corner of her forehead. The other was dangling from a hank of hair, on the level of her left ear lobe. To the onlooker, her barrettes stood, in fact, at twenty after eleven, or possibly five minutes to four. Janetta was amazed. How could Judy be staring at herself in the mirror *so hard* and yet fail to see those unbalanced barrettes? From now on, before she left for school, Janetta always checked. Every time.

Janetta had once been a baby. This was an astonishing fact for Janetta to absorb. It was too far away; it was beyond memory. But of course it was true. Everyone starts out as a baby. You don't have to be very old to know *that*. Besides, there were pictures to prove it — snapshots of her grinning through the bars of her crib; looking up at her mother's adoring face; taking her first step (Mom and Dad squatting down in front of her, arms flung out to rescue her from falling); sitting in the bathtub; laughing with her mouth wide open, no teeth in sight. She certainly looked as though she had the world by the tail. Same with the later pictures — blowing out her birthday cake candles, face ready to burst, age four; swinging in the old tire, legs high in the air, age five; on Bayswater Beach, lying flat on her stomach in the wake of a spent wave, age six; eating cotton candy at the fair, eyes wide, her mouth lost behind a pink beard, age seven.

Best of all Janetta liked the one in which her mother was looking adoringly at her. She was cradling her in her arms (age five months? Who can tell?) and gazing down at her. Her mother was very young and pretty, and in her eyes was such an aching expression of love that when Janetta looked at it, she could feel her eyes stinging at the corners. She also liked the cotton candy picture, but she didn't know exactly why. Maybe because of the day, which Janetta could remember so clearly. Her father took the picture (and another blurry one of her on the merry-go-round), and no one else was there. It was like a miracle to have him all to herself. Mom was at home, throwing up.

That was the start. She threw up a lot, and not just in the morning. Often she lay down in a curled-up ball, facing the wall, not even looking at anybody. That lying-down thing seemed to go on forever and ever. Janetta would watch her from the doorway, wanting to go in, not daring to. Her mother seemed like a whole new person. Janetta didn't know what the ground rules were anymore.

Her father told her, "Mom's feeling pretty awful. Try not to bother her too much."

Once she said to her mother, "Could we go down to Point Pleasant Park and look for some ducks to feed?"

Her mother's eyes were sad and unfocused. "I'm sorry, sweetie," she said, and gave her hand a squeeze. "Not today. I feel too terrible." She shut her eyes. "I just feel like I'm dying." Then she got up very quickly and went off to the bathroom to be sick again.

Dying! Janetta watched the closed bathroom door and willed it to open. Then her mother came out and lay down again on the sofa, very pale. "Be patient," she said, her voice very low and hoarse. "This is only supposed to go on for three months.

Then we'll go to the park. We'll do all sorts of wonderful things. Just wait. You'll see." She reached out her arm and gave Janetta a limp hug.

Three months. Another forever. Could you get over dying in three months? But it wasn't three months. It was five. "Just wait," she'd said. Janetta often felt like crying, but she couldn't. If she upset her mother, maybe she wouldn't just *feel* like dying. She could hear her father saying, "Try not to bother her too much." And she couldn't bother *him*. He seemed to be away most of the time.

Then Janetta's mom got bigger and bigger, until Janetta could hardly believe that anyone could be that huge without bursting. She knew, of course, that there was a baby in there — two babies, in fact — but she would have believed it if someone had told her that there were actually four. No wonder her mother was tired. What must it be like lugging around that great big body every single day?

A couple of times, Janetta said to her mother, "Are you ready to go to the park yet?" But her mother sat down and looked at her very hard, reaching out her hand to touch Janetta's cheek. "Honey," she said, "Daddy's got the car. I'd never make it down there on my own two feet. I feel like a Mack truck. Without wheels. I know it's really hard for you to understand, but I'm just so *weary*. And my back hurts a whole lot. Maybe next week. Right now I feel three-quarters dead." But next week it was the same. And when Daddy was home, he stuck so close to her mother that it was like he was scared she'd break if he left her alone for two seconds. Break or *die*.

Once Janetta's dad took her to the park, but it wasn't really any fun. He forgot the bread for the ducks, and he was so serious and silent all the time they were gone that she didn't know whether she should talk or not. Almost the only thing he said

was, "Babies can come early, you know. And that can be bad."
Bad? Why bad? It sounded good to Janetta. Let's get the whole
thing over with as fast as possible. But . . . bad. In what *way*
bad? She wanted to leave the ducks and go home. She looked
at them — mallards, mergansers — but she wasn't really
watching. They weren't reaching her. She didn't even notice the
blue sea and the big boats sliding by so silently. Usually she
loved them. Their hugeness made her breath catch. But today
she couldn't have told you what shape they were or what
colour, although she seemed to be staring at them the whole
time. But the pictures in her head were stronger, more vivid.

"Let's go home," she said to her dad. "Let's check up on
Mom."

"Good idea," he said, taking her hand.

They walked past the container port, and she didn't even
stop to marvel at the giant cranes lifting their humungous
boxes. They creaked and groaned and slid along their tracks.
She didn't look.

❉

Eventually, in mid-August, Janetta's mother went off to the
hospital, face tight, hand clutching her back, in Mrs. Simes's
car. Mrs. Simes lived next door. It was Monday, and Janetta's
father was away. He was a salesman, and during that fortnight
he was doing what he always called his "swing around New
Brunswick." His boss didn't think that having twins was a good
reason to stay home. There were all those orders. In a reces-
sion, you can't ignore orders. No siree.

The twins' delivery was complicated, and Janetta's mom had
to stay in the hospital for seven days. During that time, Janetta
lived at the Nicholsons' house. Mom's last words had been,

"Now, be a good girl at the Nicholsons. It's so kind of them to invite you. She's got four kids of her own. But that should make it fun for you." Then, just before she disappeared into the car, she called back, "Don't forget to say thank you before you leave."

Four kids. The baby was really little and seemed to cry most of the time. Even when he was asleep, he made sad whimpery noises. He didn't look one bit like Janetta's happy baby pictures. Then came Lucy, who was four. On the second day, she stood beside Janetta and watched her drawing a very beautiful picture (of her own house and tulip garden, with blue birds flying in the sky and kittens playing) which she was planning to give to her mother as a welcome-home present. Lucy took one of her crayons and made four big red scribbles across the page before Janetta even realized what was happening. She clenched her hands together to keep them from punching Lucy in the stomach. Then she went up and shut herself in their messy bathroom (towels just tossed over the racks or dumped on the floor, brown rings in the bathtub, toothpaste tubes left open and dribbling white guck over the sink, not like home) and put her forehead down on the rim of the basin. She'd like to have cried, but she couldn't. She was trying so hard to be grateful and nice that she felt stiff and tight all over. Holding all that hate inside her was seizing her right up.

Oscar Nicholson was eleven — really old. He kept a dead mouse in his pocket. When his mother was too busy to know what was going on — which was most of the time — he would often pull out the mouse and waggle it in front of Janetta, close to her face. She thought she might faint from the terror she felt. She didn't know what she was frightened of, but the fear was terrible. Her mouth was dry and she could feel a small thin scream locked in her throat, straining to get out. And when he wasn't scaring her with the mouse, she kept being afraid that he would. She had to keep watching his pocket and what his hands were doing.

But Stella was the worst. Stella was seven and a half years old — the same age as Janetta. She waited until no one else was around, and then she did or said things. On the third day, she said, "Want to play with my doll?" and held it out to Janetta, smiling. Janetta felt she needed badly to have something to hug, and reached out for it hungrily. The instant before her hands touched the doll, Stella snatched it away. "Changed my mind," she snapped, still smiling, but with her lips pressed together and ugly.

One day, when they were outside playing in the drizzle, with the foghorns moaning and lamenting down by the harbour (the weather was awful, all that week), Stella said, "Sometimes people die having babies." Another time she said, "I bet your dad won't come home again, ever. Fathers don't like having too many kids around. *Everyone* knows *that*." Or just, "It must be gross to have straight hair." Stella's was curly and glossy black.

Mr. Nicholson was either silent or crabby. It just depended. "Shut up, you kids!" he'd yell, when the noise got too wild. Mrs. Nicholson was busy. Not for one second did she stop being busy. She walked the floor with the screaming baby, looking frantic, her hair uncurled and fine, hanging in pale strings over her ears, not very clean. She served potato soup or hamburger hash or corned beef and cabbage, so there'd be only one pot to wash. She left the dirty dishes on the counter, piling up and spilling over onto the stove and the sink until there was hardly a spot on which to lay down one small teaspoon. When there were no more dishes left to use, she washed them, usually after everyone else had gone to bed for the night. Janetta listened to her down there, clattering around. Later, she could hear thunking noises in Mr. and Mrs. Nicholson's bedroom. It was hard to sleep.

During that week it often poured with rain, and the Nicholsons didn't have a dryer. Damp laundry hung from lines strung across the kitchen, sometimes even in the living room and in the back and front porches. When Stella asked her mother something like "Can you look at a picture I drew this morning?", Mrs. Nicholson would say, "Later," or "Not now. I'm too busy," or "Can't you hear the baby crying?" Everywhere you looked, toys littered the floors — torn books, blocks, rattles, naked dolls, balls to trip over. Lucy poked the sleeping baby and the screams began anew. Oscar slapped Lucy, who went and threw Stella's new dinosaur down the dirty cellar steps. Stella dragged Janetta outside on the veranda and told her that twins were often born with no feet. Mrs. Nicholson hung up yet another wash on the crowded lines, face blank.

On Saturday, Mr. Nicholson sat in the living room and watched game shows and baseball on TV, clicking back and forth on the remote, biting his nails. Once, when he tripped on one of Lucy's pull-toys, he kicked it so hard that the wheels fell off and went spinning away in all directions. Stella would come up to him and touch his hand, resting on the arm of his chair, and maybe beg, "Can we play cards?" "I'm tired," he'd say. "Don't forget it's me that makes the money around here to keep all your stomachs full of food. I'd like some peace and quiet on the weekends." Then he'd change channels and drown out her complaints with noisy commercials. Sometimes he'd call out, "When's supper?"

At night, Janetta lay wide awake, with Stella beside her on the same bed. She was afraid to move, in case Stella woke up and started to tell her more scary things, breathing her nasty night breath over her as she talked. She thought about big families, and how she was soon going to be part of one. She already knew that she had twin brothers, and that they weighed six and a quarter and six and one-half pounds, and that they had curly hair. She thought about the twins' feet. She heard snores and snuffling coming from the other rooms. She believed that her father would come home, but she didn't know this for absolute sure. She remembered the day at the fair, and the cotton candy. She could taste the sweetness of it, and the wispy weightlessness. She knew that her mother hadn't died yet, but maybe that happened later, after babies were out of their mothers, and older. She wanted to cry, but she couldn't. Crying can be noisy, and Stella might wake up. Better to clamp her teeth together and hold her breath until the feeling passed.

✳

On Monday of the next week, Mrs. Nicholson spoke to Janetta as she was pushing her cornflakes around the bowl.

"Your mother's coming home today," she said. "Mrs. Simes is bringing her back at ten-thirty. Better get your stuff ready. Your pyjamas and all. Mrs. Simes'll phone for you when they get there." Why Mrs. Simes? Why not her mother? Never mind. If her mother was coming home, she must be alive, but maybe too far gone to use the telephone. Sick or something. But not dead.

Mrs. Nicholson continued. "When you're ready, go on outside and play with Stella until it's time to leave."

But Stella didn't wait. She grabbed Janetta's hand — too tight, as usual. She pulled her outside and shoved her onto the huge back-porch swing, pushing the floor until it started to move, higher and higher, back and forth.

"Mothers like boys better than girls," she shouted above the squeaky mechanism.

"They don't, either," Janetta said, very low.

But Stella heard her. "Do, too," she hollered. "I got brothers. I *know*. My mom likes them way best. Besides . . ."

"Besides what?" Janetta was yelling now, too.

"When you're almost eight, you're not cute anymore. That's what parents really like. They want their kids to be little and cute and cuddly."

Janetta looked down at her dumpy legs. She felt very tired. "I gotta go in and pack," she said. She checked the time on her Mickey Mouse watch, her father's present for her seventh birthday. "It's almost ten."

"Stupid-looking baby watch," Stella said, and jumped off, leaving Janetta to clatter back and forth on the massive metal swing until it finally stopped. "Hurry up, slowpoke!" she shouted from inside the house.

Janetta went up the stairs one step at a time, feet heavy. She packed her things into her plastic Sobey's bag — her pyjamas and slippers, her extra underpants, her toothbrush, her stuffed bear. The bear had a black ear now, from the day Lucy attacked him with a black crayon. (Lucy almost never went anywhere without her crayons.) Janetta took the bag and went into the bathroom, locking the door behind her. Maybe she could cry, now. If she did, perhaps that squeezed feeling in her chest would go away. But she couldn't. Stella was outside, pounding on the door and yelling, "Gotta go! Gotta go! I'm gonna wet my pants!" Janetta opened the door and walked out. When she was able to get back in, the crying feeling was gone.

❊

At 10:30 sharp, the phone rang. Janetta, normally slow moving, shot forward to answer it. The voice at the other end said, "Please tell Janetta she can come home now and see her new brothers."

"I'm Janetta," she said, but Mrs. Simes had already hung up.

Janetta flew out the door. The Sobey's bag flapped against her legs as she raced down the street. Her house was only two blocks away, but at the end of the first block she suddenly stopped. She stood there for a moment or two, perfectly still, and then she turned around and ran all the way back to the Nicholsons. She dashed in the front door without knocking. The baby was in his carriage, crying; Lucy was watching cartoons on TV, with the sound turned up to full volume, peeling the paper off a red crayon; Stella and Oscar were fighting over a game of Monopoly, throwing around houses and hotels. Janetta found Mrs. Nicholson out by the washing machine, stuffing dirty laundry into the top.

"Thank you very much," Janetta panted, "for the lovely time."

Then she was gone. In three minutes she was home. At the bottom of the steps she stopped to catch her breath. Boys better than girls. No feet. Too many kids around. Won't come home again, ever. Sometimes die. Cute and cuddly. Straight hair. Slowly she walked up the stairs. She stopped again at the top, and took another deep breath. Then she reached out her hand and opened up her own front door.